# Travel is a Dubious Delight

## Sue Eltringham

I owe a great deal to the kindness of friends who agreed to read the stories, to make suggestions and to look for mistakes in spelling, word order, punctuation and much more. They found them in abundance. The book would be in a really bad state without the help of John Cooter-Baker, Prue Harrison, Alan Hodgson, Nichola Rodgers and Véronique Garnier-Clair. Thank you all for your contributions and for your most kind words of encouragement.

I would also like to thank Jenny Hewitt for her great patience, perseverance and kindness in acting as a publisher's go-between and a cover designer.

Without her help, all would have gone astray.

In memory of Keith Eltringham who wrote books about elephants and hippos and conservation.

All proceeds in aid of: The George Adamson Wildlife Preservation Trust (GAWPT)

Charity number 279598

# 1 The First Leg of the Journey

At Waterloo Station the machine stamped Sarah's Eurostar ticket and she lugged her case of samples through to the security check. Beside her, a couple was having problems. An official hurried to assist. What could there be inside the pear-shaped canvas bag? Curiosity made x-raying an imperative and there on the screen was the skeleton of a small animal.

'Taxidermist?' enquired the x-ray man.

The couple went to stare. Then the woman gasped: 'It's the cat!' and she turned accusingly to her partner in his Paris-visiting suit. 'Geoffrey, you swore you'd shut her in the utility room! Poor Whimsy must have suffocated.'

Without a second's thought, the bag was unzipped. Long blond hair curtained her face, as the woman leaned forward to lift out the limp furry body but the cat revived, shot out between her arms and vanished.

Sarah moved on. She could hear Geoffrey trying to calm his anguished Leonie: 'Cats find their way home.' There was much contacting of neighbours on mobile phones.

Later, when everyone gathered to board the train, the couple was just ahead of Sarah in the queue, waiting to enter the coach she was booked on. The woman, Leonie, bravely flicked back her hair, demonstrating the great resilience of her character. She was carrying the pear-shaped bag because Geoffrey was using a walking stick. –He gripped the handrail to pull himself up the steps of the coach. Sarah waited behind him, but, although the dark brown trouser-leg in front of her began to rise up with the rest of his suit, a polished left shoe remained stuck to the platform. A lump of chewing gum, she assumed vaguely, until she saw a fawn sock and a length of pale leg emerge from the bottom of the trouser-leg. Soon there was an almost complete leg resting against the coach steps just in front of Sarah.

As a child, she had not believed her teacher when she told the class that a beautiful butterfly would emerge from the brown chrysalis. Later, she had found one in the garden and had hoped it would turn into a blue and yellow swallowtail but instead it had hatched out into a scream-hideous insect. Life had been full of surprises then. Now nothing amazed her.

With difficulty she grasped the leg just under its knee, intending to hand it up to its owner but Geoffrey seemed not to have noticed his loss.

The most sinister surprise of all, she recalled, had been when she and a friend explored some woods on a chalky hillside. From the outside all seemed normal but once they had pushed their way beneath the outer leaves, inside the wood, every twig was brown, no leaf grew: the whole wood was still as death.

By the time Sarah had heaved up her case of samples and climbed aboard, still clutching the leg, its owner had moved on. She felt mildly disconcerted but judged he could not have got far with only one leg. That business with the cat was pre-occupying him, she guessed. Even so, it was strange that he had not noticed his leg was missing. Perhaps, she reasoned, Geoffrey was in the habit of swinging himself around his home and garden without the weight of the artificial limb. He probably wore it only on formal occasions and felt more normal without it.

Sarah stowed her case and looked down at the leg. So, it was true: Lost Property Offices really did contain items like this. She draped her coat over the leg and walked down the carriage carrying it in front of her like a standard lamp. The weight of her coat made her fingers ache and her grip on the knee began to slip so she rested the leg against her shoulder and held onto the socked ankle. The short length of inner thigh rested intimately against her cheek - but it was wrapped in her coat, of course.

Two people were reading the Times and the Telegraph and she was certain they must be Geoffrey and Leonie but when she came up to them, the man was wearing two black shoes. She reached the end of the coach without finding the one-legged man.

Suppressing the vaguest twinge of surprise, Sarah naturally assumed they'd gone to the restaurant car for breakfast. She made her way through another coach, glancing down at people's feet all the way in case there was a match for the left shoe digging into her ribs. By the time she reached the restaurant car the train was well into its journey. Geoffrey and Leonie were not waiting for their breakfast.

She went the full length of the train in both directions and then returned to her seat to decide what to do next. She might have missed seeing them. She would ask the guard to make an announcement. It was awkward not knowing their surname but they would guess at once what it was about. 'Would Geoffrey and Leonie please go to seat number 14 in coach B.'

Then she remembered how surprised she had been when the special constable, whom she had asked for help, had accused her of stealing a suitcase. He informed her that she should immediately hand over all lost property to the correct authority. All she'd been trying to do was save time and exchange the suitcase in her possession for her own case, similar in size and colour, which she'd seen some idiot pick up by mistake from the luggage rack on the tram. He'd leaped off, quick as a flash, and hurried away with it.

'I yelled out to him and I tried to run after him,' she explained to the policeman, 'but his suitcase weighs a ton. It must be full of books. You'd think he would have noticed the difference. He's either going to the bus station or the YMCA.' The constable took the suitcase on the crossbar of his bike. 'How will I recognise this man?' asked the policeman. 'He'll be carrying a suitcase like this one, only slightly smaller, a lot lighter and a brighter navy blue.' Happily, the exchange was made on the steps of the YMCA where the confused student had just discovered his mistake and didn't quite know what to do about it. The constable rode back to her in triumph with her suitcase, and so Sarah was able to catch her train.

The artificial leg was not her responsibility, after all. She wondered if the way she was deliberately concealing the leg with her coat might look suspicious if she ever had to defend her actions in court. Even so, she could not bring herself to remove the coat in front of the other people in the coach. In a minute or so, once her fellow travellers had settled down and become rather less alert, she'd take the thing along to the end of the carriage and dump it in the luggage space.

She wondered about the strange absence of the couple and came to the conclusion that they must, in fact, have got off the train again, either to look for the leg or because they'd received a message on the mobile about their cat. It seemed impossible that they could have slipped by her while she was putting her case in the luggage rack so they must have left the coach by the other door. An odd thing to do but then they were upset about the cat.

Sarah took out her book. The Kent countryside hurried by the window. The leg would be found in Paris. Some Eurostar cleaner would hand it in to Lost Property.

She could not concentrate on her book with the leg nudging her knee. Perhaps Geoffrey and Leonie had intended to leave the leg on the train? That business with the cat seemed most peculiar, even though cats do creep into boxes and confined places. Perhaps this live cat distraction was a way of smuggling something into France: the prototype of an artificial limb, for example. She lifted up the corner of her coat and peeped at it. Then it occurred to her that the leg might contain a bomb. She listened to hear if it was ticking. The train would soon be arriving at Ashford. She ought to alert the security guards. They would question her. She would probably be taken off the train to examine police photographs of suspected terrorists. She would miss her vital appointment. Her business would suffer irreparable harm. She decided to get rid of the leg.

In the toilet she had great difficulty opening the ventilation panel. It took her a long time but eventually, by using the brown-shoed foot as a lever, she managed to make an opening large enough to force the leg through. She flung it as far away from the track as she could. It disappeared into the long grass. She returned to her seat with her coat over her arm just as the train began to slow down.

The stop in Ashford seemed unusually long. What could be causing the delay? Surely no one had seen her poking the leg out through the window? Did they have security cameras in the toilets? If it were a bomb timed to explode inside the tunnel, the train really should be getting as far away from the prosthetic leg as possible. She began to get agitated. People were staring at her. She'd made a horrendous moral blunder. No question about it. She should have been prepared to sacrifice her business for the sake of the public good. It was just the sort of selfish act she was always condemning others for. If it were a bomb, she would be morally obliged, always supposing she survived the blast, to come forward and help the police with their enquiries. She would have to admit everything. They probably wouldn't believe her. They'd question her ex-boyfriend. She was leaning forward breathing heavily, elbows on her knees, face buried in her hands.

'Are you all right?' the girl next to her asked.

'Yes,' she whispered, thinking what a stupid question to ask when she was obviously distressed. 'I just wish they'd start the train.'

'There's nothing to be nervous about. I've been through the tunnel many times.'

'So have I,' croaked Sarah.

At last the train started and they were soon passing under the English Channel. Sarah relaxed. She smiled at her own stupidity; fancy thinking the leg had contained anything explosive - it had weighed almost nothing. The French countryside, so like that of Kent, was flashing by at high speed.

Sarah had become engrossed in her book when she suddenly became aware of a man striding up the corridor shouting something in French: had anyone lost... Sarah looked up. Above his head he was holding up an artificial leg. She squirmed lower in her seat. She couldn't even bring herself to verify whether the brown shoe was a left or a right one.

# 2  The Magic of Crossing Water

We call them boats because it makes them seem small and friendly. The boating lake is shallow with an almost negligible risk of drowning, for adults anyway. 'Ships' is what sailors go on. They sail across the 'High Seas'. One must be intrepid to venture there. The very words conjure a tang of vomit.

As children we often got taken down to the riverside to watch the ships. In those days long, high ships loomed past on their way to London Docks. The river was always busy then, with clouds of black smoke rolling out of scarlet funnels and much tooting by tugboats and smaller craft as they dodged in and out between the startlingly deep-throated liners and cargo vessels. From Grandpa we learned to recognise ensigns and foreign flags, (*'Does that flag mean she wants a pilot, Grandpa?'*) and which ships belonged to which shipping lines from the colours painted on their funnels. Grandpa also invented stories for us about their cargoes and destinations. (*'But Grandpa, what's she carrying to Trincomalee?' 'Grandpa, where do the sailors keep their hats?' 'Hats?' 'On that ship from Panama?'*) We'd watch the river pilots heavily climb up the ladders fixed to the cliff-like sides of the ships, or the tugboats nuzzle the bigger ships into Tilbury docks. After such a beginning how could one not nurse a passionate desire to be aboard and away with the fast emptying tide?

All this travelling about seems to be as much a part of human behaviour as migrating is for some species of birds, at least it is for some members of our human race. Or maybe it is simply a highly contagious disease, a sea fever.

People living near the coast have always gone to sea, fishing, whaling, or plundering the wealth of other coastal dwellers. When we were children, explorers like Columbus, Magellan, Drake and Cook were romantic heroes and we too longed for sea adventures.

We used to go across the ferry to Tilbury, a trip I can highly recommend as having all the best aspects of a sea voyage, without any of its disadvantages. It was fairly cheap for a start. In fact, now I come to think of it, I cannot imagine how any seafarer could possibly desire anything more. They say all ports are the same the world over so why not keep going back and forth to Tilbury?

It was perfect. As children, we enjoyed an anticipation almost as intense as if we were going on a world cruise. The luggage needed on the voyage had to be discussed, (*'Oh no, I haven't got to wear that old raincoat-thing I wear to school every day! Mu-um, it's horrible.'*) caps, scarves, gloves, extra cardigans perhaps, because the wind could feel like a whetted knife coming up the estuary and across the marshes.

There was the walk (*'Stop skipping about.'*) down the steep, narrow High Street to the river. Sometimes a moored ship quite filled the end of the road, taller than the roofs of the shop-houses. How unbearably itchy our woollen socks became (*'Stop fidgeting. Stand properly'*) during the age it took to buy the tickets! How the distant smell of sea water, considerably diluted by pollution, though nobody knew about such things in those days, lured us through the creaky turnstile! The little pier building was echoingly empty except for a weighing machine and a strong smell of public lavatories, undiluted by sea water. Why could we not go through and out onto the floating landing stage NOW? (*'Oh Mu-um, ple-ease!'*)

An unendurable wait, the agony was indescribable, (*'Oh, for goodness' sake! Do stand still, can't you?'*) then at last we were out on the floating pier in the bright light reflected off the river. Not having found our sea legs yet, we walked in a strange way about the huge, floating raft, which had ropes round it to keep you from falling in. (*'Keep away from the edge.'*) There were great hoops of red and white life belts hanging about ready to throw in after you in case you did. How the water kept moving all the time, flicking itself up in the air as though trying to jump up and reach you! (*'Come away from the edge, you two. Didn't you hear me? You'll fall in if a big wave comes along.'*) How erratically the raft bobbed up and down when the long curling bow-wave of a ship came skimming towards us over the water! We watched it lap high up the seaweed-draped iron legs that supported the real pier and then waited for the wave to come washing back again off the river-wall.

A long way across the water was Tilbury and it took concentrated searching to pick out the other ferry boat, (*'Oh yes. There she is! I can see her now.'*) the one we were soon going to board, having missed the earlier ferry. There she was, just pushing out from the opposite shore. We awaited Minnie (*'I do hope it's Minnie. They can't call the other one Mickey because it's a boy's name.'*) with much anxiety. Would she manage to avoid collision with the empty cargo vessel coming down in the centre of the river on the ebbing tide at a great rate of knots, her plimsoll line high above the water? It was a worrying few moments till the ship had gone by. Then there was the ferry again, very dumpy-looking as she buffeted across in a wide arc (*'Oh, Mu-um, it's Rosa not Minnie coming for us! '*) because of the pull of the current.

With hardly a bump, although she could have bumped as much as she liked because she had so many splendid fraying rope fenders as well as old motor tyres hung around her, Rosa slid alongside the floating jetty. Sometimes, when half a gale was blowing, the ferry had trouble getting alongside, whilst in very thick fog, the service might be withdrawn, in spite of radar.

We stood back (*'Stand over here, and keep out of the way, for goodness sake.'*) and admired the way the ropes were flung and caught by men in navy jerseys. Their performance may not have been quite as spectacular nor have had quite the same dramatic effect as that of a rope snaking down through the air from the deck of the Queen Elizabeth but it was still very impressive. The rope had to be caught first time and swiftly wrapped two turns round a bollard to take the strain - if not, the ferry might be swept out of reach. Sometimes there was much revving of the noisy engine to get the ferryboat properly adjusted into the required position. Then, with quick swirling movements, the ropes were unwound to be rewound tighter and more securely so that the gangways could be run out. (*'Hoy! Mind yer backs there!'*)

Sometimes, depending on the tide, the gangway down onto the floating jetty was impressively steep, (*'Stop running, you'll fall over.'*) but the gangplanks from the floating jetty onto the ferry only moved up and down a little with the weight of the passengers. Some passengers who were in a hurry didn't wait for the gang planks but jumped the bobbing gap like real sailors. (*'No, no, come back, you can't do that. Here, hold my hand.'*)

All the disembarking passengers were off now and at last we were allowed to walk up the gang plank and onto the boat. (*'Oh Mum, isn't this LOVELY, Mum?'*) Our trip across the water would soon begin.

The excitement and activity before the departure of the ferry rivalled that of any ocean-going liner, with the added attraction that it would not be followed by an abysmally tedious, and perhaps rough, sea voyage. The length of the trip across the river was ideal. No sooner had we waved goodbye to the unfamiliar river-side view of our home-town than, (*'Come on, quick, let's go up the front end.' 'The bow, stupid!'*) just a few minutes later, we were involved in the thrill of sighting the distant landing stage, which as it came closer, appeared larger so we could see more and more fascinating details. (*'I think that's a dog waiting to come on the ferry.' 'No it isn't. They don't let dogs come on here, because, in case they fall in the river.' 'Yes they do. It is a dog, isn't it, Mum?' 'No, it isn't, stupid. Come on, let's go down these stairs.' 'Don't run, you'll fall.'*)

There was no time to get fed up with the limited space and facilities on board. The engine, with its smell of boiling oil, and truly deafening pounding, which caused the whole vessel to quake with paroxysms of juddering, was the most terrifying thing I have ever encountered. (*'She's frightened, but I'm not frightened.'*) We had to go past it to get to the stairs leading back up on deck. It took courage, backed by a certain degree of curiosity, to linger near the throbbing heart of the ship and peer through the metal grill at the dark, quivering, oily metal shapes. *('I like the noise. I'm going to stay here all the time and watch the engine.' 'Come along, will you. You'll get lost, lagging behind like that.')*

The inside lounge and saloon were also distasteful because of the unbreathable dense cigarette smoke and the chink of thick glasses. *('We aren't allowed in the boozer, are we Mum?' 'Shush! I don't know where you get these words, I'm sure.' 'But Dad always ...' 'That's quite enough from you, young man.')*

On deck it was clear and bright and wonderful, though cold. It was impossible to find a place out of the wind, try as we might. Wreathed in smiles, *('Isn't this LOVELY, Mum?')* teeth chattering with cold, we used to sit on hard, brown-painted, slatted wooden benches. These were designed to float off the deck in the event of a shipwreck. The ropes, which were looped round them so that you could hang onto them in the water, were useful for resting the heels of your sandals in when your legs got tired of dangling.

If we were going ashore, instead of just doing the round trip, then we suffered the almost uncontrollable delight *('There's no need to rush. Now just wait. Here, take my hand. Let's wait for those idiots in a hurry to get off first.')* of going down the gang plank onto terra firma in another county, Essex, where they speak a queer version of English, quite different from our Kentish-cockney.

When we were older and our first teeth were at a critical stage, *('It's just hanging on by a thread.' 'No, no don't touch Mum. Mu-um, that HURTS!')* the Birthday Treat was extended to include the taking of tea, toasted teacakes (or if not available: toast) and strawberry jam in the Tilbury railway station's Silver Tea-Room. *('It's my birthday, so I can choose first.')* But we always had the same. On at least three occasions we or our friends were proud to lose one of our wobbly front teeth in valiant tussles with the incredibly rubbery, yet delicious, toast of the Silver Tea-Room.

*'Hey, d'you want to know a magic way of pulling out your teeth?'* we'd ask our friends. *'You have to go across water or it doesn't work.'*

# 3 Don Quixote in Seville

The buses in Seville are jolly places where there is more standing room than sitting. One of the pleasures of standing is that everyone gets thrown up against everyone else whenever there is an urgent, or extremely urgent, need to brake. In Seville, there are plenty of emergency stops during even the shortest ride, but the people accept this constant careering into their neighbours, and the quite painful foot-trampling that ensues, with stoical good grace. Of course, there can be moments of delightful, hands-on intimacy, but normally, it is a case of those enormous handbag-weapons women carry, catching you in the ribs.

Chivalry is not yet dead in that country of Don Quixote, and especially not in the romantic southern city of Don Juan. However, in the example I witnessed, its lasting as far as the city centre seemed precarious.

What do you do when a gentleman offers you his seat?

(This is so rare an occurrence in England now - Women's Lib seems to require virile men to trample underfoot pregnant and aged females - that one has lost the art of gracious acceptance. Only newly arrived immigrants attempt this courtesy on the London Underground.)

I learned too late what one should do in Spain. I actually saw it enacted on the very same bus route a few days later. An elderly gentleman got up to offer his seat to a middle-aged lady. She firmly refused and continued to decline his offer, in spite of much impassioned pleading. She shook her head, flapped her hand, (the one she wasn't holding on with) and shouted at her would-be knight over the clattering of the engine. Their fervent exchange would have made a splendid operatic libretto. Imagine it sung in Italian:-

"Pray do me the honour."

"No thank you, sincerely."

"I beg you, madam."

"No, no. Too kind."

"I insist."

"I cannot."

"How can you refuse me?"

"I'm getting off at the next stop."

"Even so ..." etc etc.

All the while this continued across the width of the bus, the courteous gentleman remained on his feet, arguing and wobbling as the driver did jerky battle with the gears. Finally he over-balanced and flopped back into his seat, defeated.

I ought to have dealt equally firmly right from the start with my seat-offerer. My feeble excuse is that shouting in buses is not the northern European way, and anyway, he probably wouldn't have understood my poor Spanish. Perhaps I should simply have flapped my hand nonchalantly and turned to stare out of the window, but then he might have tugged my sleeve... Even now, knowing the dire consequences, could I really have been that uncivil?

My initial mistake, the root-cause of my predicament, was committed on entering the bus. It is a perfect example of how NOT to behave in a foreign country. It is of the utmost importance that foreigners watch what the locals are doing and merge. Spit if they spit, forbear to touch if they don't, kiss when they kiss, roll about on the football pitch in pretended agony if that's what's expected, in short, when in Rome do as the Romans do, even if it's against your nature. It's so arrogant of us to impose our now-meaningless ethnic hand-shaking, or whatever we consider to be 'good-manners', on foreign societies. If they thumb their noses at you, don't be inhibited: do it back!

Alas, I did not conform to the local bus customs and as a result suffered an excruciating, long-drawn-out embarrassment.

On the buses in Seville, people just shuffle past the ticket-punching machine and hang on to the nearest seat-back. This is what everyone does, so you must do it too - not what I did, which was to move swiftly to the back of the bus where there was no one near enough to fall against. My motive was purely altruistic. It just seemed a good idea to move along so that people coming onto the bus after me wouldn't have to push through the tightly packed crush just inside the door. I was stupid not to realise that people actually enjoy other people's pushing past as they clog up the passage. They get a kick (often literally) from the intimacy of having people falling on top of them and laddering their tights.

The elderly gentleman must have assumed that I'd ventured to the far end of the bus in search of an empty seat, and when so charming and neatly turned-out an old gentleman courteously saluted me and offered me his seat - how could I have forced myself to simply turn away and pretend I hadn't noticed?

*He does not remember he is old*, I thought, whilst having to come to terms with the bitter fact that I must look terribly ancient myself for him to offer his seat to me. How could he guess what strong and hefty thighs I have, nor how well they're suited to adjusting to the bucking rough-ride of this bus?

With my most dazzling smile I thanked him and accepted his kind offer. Only as the bus cavorted off, did I realise how thin and weedy his thighs were inside his beautifully pressed trousers.

I assumed he would get off at the next stop. I thought that my gratitude and smile had been purchased by the fairly cheap device of rising early: a tactic often employed to give oneself a good start in the tottering race for the door as the vehicle pounces to a halt.

Out of the corner of my eye, I watched him as he clung on with both hands to the upright post. He swayed about a good deal and seemed to retrieve his balance only at the very last moment. He was obviously not an experienced bus-stander. I glanced ahead trying to estimate how many intersections the driver would have to negotiate before the next bus stop. Would the old man's legs hold out? Would he crack his head on the upright bar? Should I get up and offer him his seat back again?

Impossible. His carefully barbered face gave no indication of panic. The aristocratic nose was proud, the intelligent mouth most serious. He had given up his seat to a foreign lady thus demonstrating that chivalry is not dead in Seville.

The bus stop came. He did not get off. I shot him an accusing look. His erect head, its thin grey covering well-trimmed, was turned away from me.

You villain, I thought, you have deceived me.

I was only too well aware that the closer we came to the city centre the more the sudden, jolty brake applications would increase. I resorted to praying that he would get off at the next stop.

By a stroke of luck not to be missed by the driver, the bus found itself on an empty expanse of tarmac. This happened to be where the road swerves to avoid a tumbling fountain which stands in the centre of a great convergence of many traffic routes. The driver joyfully accelerated into this space so that we spun, carousel-fashion, around the fountain. This provided the standing passengers with the thrill of keeling over and leaning against one another - or, for those with no one handy, of stumbling several totters to the right.

Don Quixote clung on gallantly for dear life while his neat, well-polished shoes performed a rapid little skipping dance. Was there, upon that solemn countenance, the faintest glint of triumphant self-satisfaction at finding that he had survived the driver's attempt to unfoot him?

I noted, however, when the vehicle eventually resumed a straight course, that his feet were set more widely apart and his knees were bent, the better to absorb the shocks caused by all the little avoidance dashes and panic stops dictated by traffic conditions.

He was bound to dismount at the next stop, I told myself. The coach-station was always popular.

But he didn't. The door closed and I'd left it too late to make a run for it. I debated whether to get up now and prepare to leave the bus at the next stop. Would it be too blatant a ruse for returning him to the safety of his seat? Surely if I'd intended my bus-ride to be that brief, I would never have accepted his offer in the first place? I watched his knuckles turning white on the upright bar. Grim determination tensed the line of his noble mouth.

It was obvious that his action had not been motivated by any desire to 'pick me up'. He'd made no attempt to engage me in conversation. Even now, his self-sacrificial eyes refused to meet mine, so how could I jokingly suggest that we take it in turns and share the seat? Beads of perspiration were, I was convinced, breaking out on the parchment skin of his forehead. Oh poor Don Quixote! Surely his Lady Dulcinea or a practical Clarrie Grundy type, would leap up, kiss him on both cheeks and sit him down. Why didn't I do that? For goodness sake, surely he'd leave at the Cathedral stop?

No such luck. What were the other passengers thinking of me for having taken the seat of this frail invalid? I dare not catch anyone's eye. At the next stop, surely he'd have to throw in the towel. His strength couldn't possibly hold out much longer. He probably suffered from some heart condition - these foreigners all smoke too much. His face had taken on a look of strained concentration. The floor of the bus bounced and reared as though we sailed a choppy sea.

What should I do if he collapsed? I'd be morally obliged to administer mouth to mouth resuscitation. I groaned and surmised that, when he did finally quit the bus, he'd be so shaky from all his exertions that he'd fall down the steps and break a hip. The crowd would probably turn on me, hurling abuse if not fists.

I squirmed. At every jolt of the bus I suffered with him. Then, in self-defence, my sympathy turned to sadistic fascination. The dotty old crow had no right to put me in this excruciating dilemma, just because I was considerate enough not to embarrass him by offering him his perch back. It was ridiculous. How was I to know, just from a casual glance, that he was going to find it quite such an ordeal to remain on his feet? Whoops, that was quite a nasty bang on the head from the metal pole. That'll teach him. All this chivalry nonsense! Next time he feels inclined to flaunt his male ego, he'll think twice. Gosh, he nearly lost his grip then. That injection of fuel seemed a bit unnecessary; only the rapid forwards tap-dancing of his twinkling toes prevented him from sitting down on the metal clasp of a large handbag on the lap of the woman beside him.

At the first whiff of spring they think they're attractive again. I ground my teeth, hating him - and myself.

His eyes were beginning to water with fear that he couldn't take much more. The proud head was upright no longer. It was difficult to tell, but I suspected that his shins were shaking with exhaustion. Lady Dulcinea/Clarrie Grundy, where are you? Poor old Don Quixote needs rescuing.

One hand slipped off the pole. His knee hit the seat strut. He was drooping to almost half his height. Like shuttlecocks in a cardboard tube, passengers were thrown backwards and forwards as the driver edged into the line of traffic. I could hear heavy breathing, little gasps and wheezes. It was probably his asthma coming on.

Really, I shouldn't have been beating up an old man like that. It was attempted murder, grievous bodily harm. Did his chivalry require him to martyr himself? Oh well, I shrugged, it was not up to me to deprive his soul of its redemption, stupid old goat! Why should I be feeling so guilty when all I'd done was flatter his male ego, a common-enough lubricant for many transactions?

Ah ha, that was it. I was being punished, by some female god maybe, for playing a dishonest game. I too suffer from pride and would rather pass out in the stuffy commuter train than ask someone to open a window or beg a seat. Blast his stupid old chivalry.

Don Quixote was about to fall over – there was nothing for it… I leaped to my feet and was about to grab him and force him back into his accursed seat, when I was beaten to it by Dulcinea in the form of the woman opposite who tapped him on the arm and pointed to her empty place as she veered, ship-board high-seas fashion, towards the group of passengers supporting each other as they waited to topple themselves off the bus at the next stop.

My heart was in my mouth as he calculated the steps needed to cross the bus and reach safety. Would he make it? The bus seemed to have reached some tranquil backwater. Courageously he let go the post. Splayed feet carried him gingerly forward. Gnarled fingers reached out anxiously towards the free seat. He'd almost made it. Then, just as he was bending to sit, the driver braked dramatically, and Quixote's chin came into violent contact with the chrome rail along the top of the seat in front. I shut my eyes not wishing to behold his ignominious slither down to lie dazed or inert upon the wooden-ridged floor. When I opened them again, he was sitting on the seat, shaken but conscious.

For several minutes I could not bring myself to take a second glance across to where chivalrous Quixote was recovering his composure. When my hysterical smile-muscles were under control once more, I took a peep and saw how his elegance and dignity had returned. Perhaps the exercise had done him good, chivvied up the digestive juices, who knows?

# 4 Love in the Clouds

Why do people go on holiday? It must be because their everyday existence is far too comfortable and boring. They need the annual self-imposed torment to bring a sense of proportion to their lives. A holiday is like a pilgrimage where the discomfort and danger are meant to atone for past sins or for some recent self-indulgence.

Perusing glossy holiday brochures is often far more relaxing than the actual gruesome hotel experience, the sunburn, the stomach upsets, the insect bites, the rip-offs and scams etc, not to mention the over-arching tedium of the airport wait, followed by the torture of close confinement in a plane.

Waiting at an airport in the queue to check in your luggage, you eye up your fellow passengers. Is there anyone there whom you'd enjoy sitting next to for hours on end? Which is the person you'd least like to plonk down in the seat beside you: the woman with the crying baby, the red-faced football fan with an open beer can, or the grossly obese sweating lad clutching his over-sized bag of crisps?

Once in your seat you watch anxiously as one by one the least favourite of your travel companions are imposed as neighbours upon other hapless travellers. The plane is filling up and here he comes, stumbling along the aisle: the most disagreeable, most miserable-looking man in the whole airport. You hope he won't have a boarding pass with your row number. You'd seen him in the waiting area, moving about, tripping over people's feet – not apologising. His shoulders droop as though he's utterly exhausted – perhaps he's been travelling for days already. His hang-dog expression seems to indicate that he's not looking forward to the journey nor to what awaits him at his destination: criminal proceedings possibly? His dismal form shuffles closer and closer. He comes to a halt beside you and deposits his hand-luggage in the over-head locker. You prepare to adjust your grumpy expression to one of cautious welcome, but he's not looking at you, he's looking at the number of the row behind you, and in he slots, right behind your seat.

Your relief is short-lived, however, because there, waiting behind him is the overweight young man with his crisp bag. He can't fit into the seat next to you without raising the armrest. Once in and sitting down, over-lapping much of himself into your space, he manages to force down the armrest. He is not built for tourist class. He really needs two seats.

This isn't possible, you tell yourself. This isn't happening. Claustrophobia, always feebly lurking around in tourist class, begins to press closer. You close your eyes and wish there was an injection they'd give you to blot out the whole journey.

You open your eyes because something is happening to the rolls of flesh: they're going. The attendant has found Fatty a wider seat up in business class or somewhere.

For a while you hope you might enjoy the luxury of an empty seat beside you but at the last minute, just as your captain is apologising for the delayed departure, issuing warnings about the risk of turbulence and predicting a time of arrival, a young girl bustles along and after a short greeting she settles down next to you and, equipped with eye-mask and blanket, she immediately falls asleep. No plastic tray of food for her then.

After a film and food, you try to sleep but suddenly you are aware of a conversation taking place behind you and it is so interesting you struggle to catch every word. Surely that vivacious, charming voice can't belong to the old Misery-guts sitting behind you? Who is he talking to? You'll just simply have to get up and go to the loo to have a proper look. It takes some thought as well as gymnastic skill to get out over the sleeping girl, but it's worth the effort.

When you get back you stand for a while, hoping the girl will wake up and let you in and while you wait you take a good look. The woman who has brought the middle-aged codger back to life is sitting beside the window in the seat behind your partner.

She notices you gawping and gives you a small smile. Her eyes are the colour of love-in-a-mist, as blue as the silk scarf she's wearing. She reminds you of your music teacher whose blue eyes always befuddled and confused your fingers. She's not saying much but nods occasionally and fixes the man in the tweed jacket with a most sympathetic love-in-a-mist gaze.

As for him... you'd never know it was the same chap. He's alert and smiling – a sparky little terrier instead of a jowly miserable bloodhound. Now he's telling her a joke, to judge by the way he laughs and she joins in. They've obviously hit it off – sometimes luck gives you a congenial companion for the flight across the Atlantic. Or maybe this is a pre-arranged, illicit holiday - two lovers not meeting up until they're on the plane and sitting together. Was all that gloomy pacing about just an act in case he was being spied on by a private detective?

You can't hear what he's saying and you can't attempt to lipread his words because he's turned towards her, fully engaged in entertaining her. You must return to your seat and slope it back to catch the snatches of conversation again. It's tricky clambering over the sleeping girl – thank goodness for your long legs, which are normally such a problem in the middle seat on an aeroplane. Now you pretend to sleep and you listen.

If only you'd come in on the conversation earlier! It's obvious from the snippets you overhear that they didn't know each other before they met on the plane. How had the exchange been initiated? What were the opening gambits?

Not all that jaunty effervescence can be attributed to the sex-appeal of the lovely lady with the love-in-a-mist blue eyes – there's a good intake of alcohol fuelling the esprit d'amour: at least three gins and tonic, the small bottle of wine with the meal and you overheard him offer her a cognac with the coffee.

It seems that they've already established that they come from roughly the same region of the west country, maybe even from the same town because it seems they're hoping to discover some mutual acquaintance. Or at least he is. He's an avid golfer – for business reasons. He deduces that she knows some of the horsey people in the county. He almost remembers their names – you suppose she puts him right, but it's more difficult to hear what she's saying in her softly refined Scottish voice because she's further away. She doesn't say much, just enough to encourage him to reveal the more flattering parts of his life story. Though he must be telling jokes against himself because he chuckles fairly frequently and you hear her light laughter on a few occasions.

Now the main cabin lights have been switched off. Only your partner's reading-light burns on - he wants to finish the thick paperback he bought at the airport. Behind you the conversation continues but at a quieter more intimate level. You're half asleep and not really interested anyway. They're probably telling each other that they don't usually fly tourist class but being recently widowed…. They're probably going to visit family or friends… Every time you rouse from your blurry half-sleep, you are aware of the murmured conversation going on and on. They're probably checking which other countries they've both visited… More than likely they've uncovered strange coincidences… Maybe they enjoy the same type of film or opera…. It is all rather wonderful and romantic.

The lights come on and you must pull yourself together. The cabin crew are distributing some immigration forms that must be filled in. The man who's sitting behind you has ordered champagne – the pop makes you jump - and then he asks the attendant to take their photograph – you imagine the two of them beaming like love-besotted teenagers, as they hold their flutes of fizz.

Then, in case they become separated in the baggage hall and because their families will be there waiting for them… they must exchange addresses and phone numbers or emails. *We must not lose touch. You promise to meet me again very soon? On this side of the Atlantic; we mustn't wait for your return to England. You will meet me here, won't you?*

There is panic in his voice. Has she given him her real address? Has she been playing with him just to pass the time?

You wonder if he took her hand and kissed it during the night or was there a more passionate embrace? Perhaps not. Does he recall that she has revealed very little of herself while he has told her everything - as never before to a living soul. How did she manage to captivate him with her blue misty eyes? She must be skilful and accomplished in the art of seduction, you think cynically. She's another wife of Bath and he's another 'Enery the Eighth' as the old song goes: 'She's been married seven times before and every one was an 'Enery'… But who knows…?

Cupid may choose to shoot his little darts up there above the clouds just as he once did on the much longer sea crossings, why not? So you wish them well and hope they'll live happily ever after.


Anyway, now we know at least one reason why people go on holiday - or undertake a pilgrimage: it's to find a mate.

# 5  The Fixer

Jim Parker had been fiddling with pliers, screwdrivers and the oilcan for almost an hour but still his motorbike refused to start. He'd have to call the garage and catch the bus into work.

"I can fix it for you." A tall, slim girl wearing motorcycle garb was silhouetted in the doorway of his garage. She stepped inside and took up his tools. Jim, who fancied himself as a bike mechanic, was extremely put out when the girl made a small adjustment, swung her shapely leg over his bike and started it first time.

"Thanks," he muttered and fast disappeared up the road on his clanky old machine.


On Saturday, he was trying to read the symbols on his video recorder. He lay on the carpet; in one hand, a magnifying glass; in the other, the instructions; and all the while, Puddles the cat walked up and down his back as though it were a see-saw plank laid upon the barrel of his stomach.

"Fiendishly keen eye-sight these Oriental designers," muttered Jim, up-ending himself so Puddles plonked onto the floor. He sighed; he'd given up all hope of recording the great football match.

As he left the room, a voice whispered: "Don't worry, I'll fix it."

That evening, after the important meeting, Jim came back and switched on the telly. He was amazed to see appearing on the screen the start of the international football match. He naturally assumed that somehow or another he'd managed to work the video recorder. He found some beer and settled down to enjoy the tension and excitement.

At breakfast next day, black smoke filled the kitchen, and the smoke-alarm wrought painful havoc in his head. He'd forgotten that the toaster didn't pop up.

"Don't worry, I'll fix it," a voice whispered close to his ear. The smoke alarm stopped.

Jim wrenched out the charcoaled bread and pushed down another slice. Now the toaster wasn't working at all.

"Shall I fix it then?" asked the silvery voice.

"Who said that?"

Jim bent down and stared at Puddles who was swallowing down her cat food as though someone else might want it.

"I'll fix the toaster, if you promise me something."

Jim was not going to promise anything to a disembodied voice. He peered around, searching high and low for its source.

"You never thanked me for recording the match for you, did you?"

"How can I thank someone I can't see."

"Promise me you'll always be grateful to me for what I do for you."

"Fix the toaster and I might be grateful for half an hour," hedged Jim.

There was scuffling noise inside the toaster. Could it be a cockroach or a small mouse? What flew out of the toaster looked like a dragonfly. Jim hunted under the Sunday papers for his glasses. What he saw when he put them on gave him rather a shock.

"Can't believe your eyes, huh?"

Jim turned pale and flopped into his chair almost on top of Puddles. He took off his glasses with a shaky hand and stared at the slender form suspended between the blur of rapidly beating wings. Was he really seeing a minute figure clad in a leather cat-suit? Two facetted roundels glittered like insect eyes on either side of its cap.

In his dozy, Sunday-morning haze Jim had thought perhaps the voice was some joke: a tape rigged up by his sister or the girls at work.

Alternatively, could his colleagues at the meeting have slipped something into his drink last night? Anger flared. He didn't like the way the dragonfly-thing was laughing at him, toying with him. He grabbed the newspaper and began swatting at it. Puddles jumped onto the fridge to assist and caught the full brunt of an ill-judged swipe. It was reassuring that Puddles could see the dragonfly-thing too.

The fierce air currents generated by Jim's frantic lunges seemed to upset the tiny creature which began shrieking the kind of language you would never expect a traditional fairy to know. It flitted up behind the spotlight. Jim fetched the light a blow that dislodged the last screw holding it in place. The lamp swung crazily on its flex and then went out.

"I'll fix it," offered the fairy.

"I'll fix you," yelled Jim, leaping onto a chair. "We don't want no F-ing aliens in this house, thanks very much. Just push off."

Instead of Jim's fixing the fairy, the fairy, of course, fixed Jim: his disc went. Every time he tried to move, jags of dazzling pain shot through him.

Then Puddles, still wanting to help, jumped onto his shoulders and despite Jim's gasp of agony, she continued upwards onto his head from where she thought she could leap up and catch the thing buzzing just out of reach. Beads of perspiration broke out on Jim's brow. The torture was exquisite.

It was precisely at this moment that Jim decided he must be the victim of a Candid Camera hoax. There was no other logical explanation. Some ingenious little radio-controlled toy was fluttering about his kitchen, taunting and tormenting him. Millions of viewers would laugh at his absurd antics. Where was the hidden camera, he wondered. He tried to transform his grimace of pain into something resembling a good-natured grin. The only way he might retrieve some of his dignity was to pretend he had known all along it was a hoax. All that flapping about with the newspaper had been him hamming it up for the cameras. With the cat on his head, one hand gripping the top of the fridge and a searing pain locking his back, Jim tried to remember what he'd said and done so far, and how he should continue so that his audience would see that he was just playing along with the joke.

"Okay, okay. You win." He tried to make his voice sound jovial. "I promise not to splatter you all over the ceiling." He dropped the rolled-up newspaper.

"Alien? Did you just call me an alien?" The seriously under-sized person in tiny motor-cycle garb was deeply offended. "I'll have you know I've been living here far longer than you have."

It fluttered down and came to rest on the kitchen table. It really was beautifully formed. Puddles took a great leap off Jim's head. Jim was too busy screaming in agony to see why the cat hadn't landed on top of the fairy. The violent jerk on his neck, however, seemed to have freed his spine, and he gingerly stepped off the chair. Puddles had somehow acquired another helping of breakfast.

"I'll have you know we Little People have been around for centuries."

"Is that a fact?" mused Jim. "In this house you mean?"

"First of all, we'll have to get rid of that cat. Puddles and I will never be compatible."

"On the other hand, we could get rid of you," suggested Jim.

At that, the fairy went berserk again: there was more unrepeatable language.

"What's the matter with you? Most humans would give their eye-teeth to have one of us in the house, especially someone as well-trained in modern appliances as I happen to be. In the old days, all we had to do was spin straw into gold, things like that. These days, I could, for example, give you free access to the Internet. What do you think?"

"Very impressive," said Jim. "What's in it for you? As I recall, there's always a catch: you'll be wanting to eat my first born or something."

"Only the cat." The fairy went on: "I mean, this place is an absolute tip. I could mend that dripping tap for a start."

"Thanks all the same, but Puddles and I go back a long way. You're the one who should move out."

Jim opened his paper and ignored the fairy. He thought he had acquitted himself brilliantly. Now was the time, he felt, when the Candid Camera Hoaxer should enter and explain. Nothing happened. He finished his piece of perfectly toasted toast, stopped staring at the amazing photo on page three and turned to the sports page.

Throughout the week, various things around the house got fixed but every meal-time Jim had to endure idiotic conversations with the Candid Camera toy.

"You're not taking me seriously, are you?" complained the fairy.

"I think it's time you moved out, you vicious insect," said Jim.

Because he refused to take the cat round to his sister's, the Candid Camera toy did something really nasty to poor Puddles. Jim had to take her to the vet who kept her in for observation.

"How would you manage without me?" said the fairy. "Look at all the things I've done for you."

"My wife used to say that. Just get it into your tiny head that I'm not buying a computer just so that you can play around on the Internet with all your Little People chums. Leave me alone. Go and live in a house that's already linked up with Wi-Fi."

Then the fairy began to sob so Jim went off down the pub where he confided his problem to Pete.

"Candid Camera denied everything when you phoned them, did they?" said Pete. "It's harassment though, isn't it? I'd better come round and take a look."

Naturally the dragonfly-thing refused to appear while Pete was in the house.

"You never told me you'd got a live-in girlfriend," said Pete.

"What?" Jim glanced round and for the first time noticed the pristine state of his abode. "Oh no. It's these Hoaxers. I don't even have to bother with the washing-up."

"Sounds like a good deal to me," said Pete.

While they had a beer and waited for the fairy to show up, Jim asked Pete about his computer and the Internet.

"Are you thinking of going in for one, then?" asked Pete.

"Nah. Can't even work the recording thingy. So Pete, if you were me, you'd be quite happy to have your place fixed up by some spooky, insect-type lodger?"

"What, no clearing up to do? Sounds all right. I'd give it go," said Pete.

Shortly after this, Puddles returned from the vet in good health, but the plumbing and electrical items reverted to their unfixed, dangerous state. The washing-up accumulated.

A month or so later, there was a rumour that Pete had set up an electrical repair business, concentrating on computers. One evening Jim met him in the pub.

"Pete, great to see you after all this time. You look as though you're doing all right."

"Busy defeating computer bugs and scams. Owe it all to the Little Woman, you know." Pete gave him a broad wink. "She'll be picking me up in the Mercedes."

When a tall, elegant woman, dressed in tight-fitting leather, strolled into the bar, Pete watched Jim closely for signs of recognition.

"You must remember Fay? You tried to introduce us."

Jim's elbow missed the edge of the bar, he spilt his beer and the bar-stool slipped from under him. "Oh no - my back's gone again!" he gasped.

"I'll fix it for you," said Fay, giving him a hand up. "Still not into computers then, Jim? You just don't know what you're missing."

Jim thought about this a moment. Then he muttered: " Well, I guess, it takes one bug to recognise another. Can I get you a glass of nectar?"

# 6  When in Rome

They have a good system in Rome, a kind of lottery. If you win, you travel on the buses free. If you lose, you have to pay a fine. Whether the fine is extortionate depends on the odds, that is to say, the likelihood of getting caught twice in the week. Nobody objects to paying £20 every ten days or £30 every month. After all, you may escape the fine for weeks on end. Hard cheese if you happen to get caught the only time you use a bus in three months. Serves you right for not using public transport more frequently. A fine might even encourage you to use it more often, just to recoup your losses. The more you think about this kind of gambling as a way of financing inner-city transport, the more sensible it seems.

A successful introduction of this system by London Transport needs subtlety and fine-tuning. A certain amount of research would be required to ascertain the best times of day to swoop upon certain categories of passenger

For example:- Regular commuters by bus or tube should still be given the option of buying a season ticket. However, they may prefer to add a certain frisson of excitement to the monotony of the daily commute by never knowing quite when the fine-collectors will strike. Think how alert they will be, even first thing in the morning, watching for the fine-collectors so that they can nip off the bus/tube just as he climbs aboard. It would become a constant war of nerves, similar to the primitive prey-predator relationship where each side is striving to outwit the other.

There should be no moral stigma attached to getting caught and paying up. It would be, after all, only what you rightly owed the transport company. If this method of fare collecting is properly regulated, the prey and the predator will be equally happy.

Fine-collectors (or ticket inspectors if they prefer this title) should disguise themselves as normal passengers. Depending on the time of day, they will be dressed as early-morning cleaners, office workers, school children, old-age pensioners, mothers with toddlers, unemployed persons, blind street vendors of lottery tickets, drunks, cinema-goers, late-night revellers etc. There could be a pool of disguises where the predatory fine-collectors could find something appropriate to wear.

Identification would be established by a quick flip of the lapel to reveal a 'Ya ha Gotcha' badge. Difficult-to-forge receipts would be exchanged for the correct money or a credit card. These receipts might give immunity from further fines for five days/hours, depending on the frequency and extortion level of the fine imposed.

After the collection, the fine-collectors would descend and merge into the crowd, possibly changing their appearance so that any 'stung' passengers cannot warn their friends by mobile phone to 'watch out for a woman wearing a green raincoat'.

Bribes given to officials in exchange for warnings of proposed 'swoops' will be accepted in lieu of fines or season tickets. Hard-to-forge tickets must be issued on receipt of these bribes. This method of payment may be preferred, and should be used by those of a nervous disposition or any whose delicate health makes it risky for them to participate in games of cat and mouse.

The joy of this type of public transport financing is that certain categories can be targeted at more frequent intervals. The resulting sliding scale of charges might favour old-age pensioners and children, whereas tourists should be hard hit as often as possible.

When we were in the Eternal City several years ago, the system was not exactly fit for purpose. Not only did we not get fined once, we even bought a booklet of ten tickets with the express intention of using them. I confess we were very slow at fathoming the system.

My Italian neighbour recommended August for Rome, "Everyone's away. You can cross the roads."

He was right but the buses were very full. What are they like when it isn't August?

Since that visit I've asked various friends what struck them most about that marvellous, historic, beautiful city, cradle of our civilisation etc, and many said it was the way their feet swelled up, which was consoling because at the time, I thought it was my cheap sandals.

I'd look down at my feet in amazement not believing they belonged to me, but there were so few other women about to whom they could belong. Everyone else was on the buses. If I'd known about not paying, I would have boarded the next one that stopped but as it was, I hobbled along the marble pavements marvelling at the ruins which, every few yards, poke up through the surface like enormous broken teeth.

The whole of Rome is, of course, a site of outstanding archaeological interest, which means no buried pipe or cable can be repaired without uncovering some monument. Soon there won't be room for the modern city to fit in around the ruins of the past. It's as though the old city is rising up from the grave to swallow its descendant.

Would I have remembered more about Rome's eternally long history if it hadn't been for my feet? The sky was blue and it was wonderful to feel warm. The feet, however, continued to swell so that eventually they completely blotted out triumphal arches, martyrs' churches and even the Coliseum.

A friend (not the swollen-footed one) had lent us a splendid tour guide which recommended long walks past buildings of architectural interest to various art galleries and museums. It offered splendid advice but not about feet or buses. So, in all innocence, with fragments of Italian, I eventually bought some bus tickets and I ascertained what one is supposed to do with them, which, in theory at least, is exactly what people actually do do in places like Geneva and even in Seville, namely push them into a ticket-punching machine on the bus to mark the date/time/route.

There is an horrific cautionary tale about an American visitor who inadvertently travelled on a Swiss bus without a valid ticket. She probably hoped to buy one on the bus. This was no excuse. She was efficiently brought to court and, besides paying a fine, she had to stand beside a bus stop. (Is there one specifically allocated for this in each town? They could become tourist attractions like gibbets at crossroads.) Standing for two hours reminding passengers to buy tickets before boarding the bus, oh the degradation, ignominy and shame of it! I'm sure the International Court of Justice would overturn such a harsh, inhumane punishment.

In Seville everybody punches their ticket as they enter the bus. It's so well organised and the people are so well disciplined that the system works even at rush hour.

Not so in Rome. At the bus stop, everyone bundles into the bus as fast as they can, preferably faster than the people standing in front of them. No queues here. It's elbows out and every man for himself. (Sorry, 'every person for itself'.) In the great stampede, one is swept forward through the bus away from any punching machine at the entrance, if it exists.

At the end of the journey it is the same story. As though being swept away by a strong current, one is carried out onto the hot pavements once more. There is no chance to dally with a ticket-punching machine.

'Of course, they've all got season tickets valid for three months so have no need to punch tickets,' I reasoned.

Next time I got on the bus, I took note of the position of the machine and determined that I would get to it and legalize my journey.

People were surprisingly uncooperative, as I dodged under raised hairy armpits and squeezed by trying not to graze buxom buttocks and corpulent stomachs. I got some distinctly dirty looks, almost as if I'd pinched someone's bottom - such a really unintelligent, as well as painful, piece of human behaviour.

Bottom-pinching is supposedly confined to males but the depravity must be related to the ancient habit of so-called maiden aunts who pinched the chubby cheeks, facial this time, of unfortunate nieces and nephews. The round rosiness must have been irresistible to those frustrated spinsters. Frustrated adolescent males must find the bulging contours beneath skirts and pants equally tempting. On the fruit-market stalls vendors can display notices requesting abstinence from fruit-squeezing but the girl on the tube must protect herself as best she can. Some step back, as though by accident, onto the assailant's foot. The weight is then progressively increased until the stiletto heel is bearing the full weight of the girl. No doubt bottom-pinchers are prepared for this and wear stout trainers. Other females with heavy handbags or stubby umbrellas dangling from their strap-hanging arms, suddenly swing round, as though they've just caught sight of a friend outside on the pavement (or on the station platform if on the tube.) Naturally, care should be taken not to injure innocent bystanders - court claims for damages can prove expensive if, in the crush, you mistake the identity of your assailant.

Let me continue with the account of my struggle to pay my fare in Rome: From the zeal with which I strove to obey the law, and to battle my way towards the ticket machine, some might have taken me for a German, but having set out on this tricky mission, it would have looked suspicious if I'd given up half way. I didn't want to be suspected of pick-pocketry.

At times I had to push quite hard to get through. Women stared at me in alarm, some thinking, perhaps, I wanted to get off the bus for health reasons. One made as though to ring the bell to bring the bus to an emergency halt - I shook my head energetically, smiled and pointed towards the ticket machine. She frowned and shrugged with incomprehension. I did wonder why no other passenger was taking advantage of the passage I'd cleaved through the garlic-scented strap-hangers. I started looking at people's hands. No one seemed to be holding a ticket. An inkling of the truth wriggled into my mind: no one else had a ticket.

Anyway, having, at length, reached the machine through sheer determination and will-power, I thought I may as well use it. I could feel curious eyes turned in my direction. Everyone in the bus was anxious to see what I did next. Possibly they'd never seen anyone actually use one of these machines before. From the reaction I got from the machine, neither had it. For a start, I had difficulty pushing the ticket in.

The bus came to a stop and I swear that certain passengers decided not to alight but instead chose to remain on the bus just to watch the end of the saga.

I eventually did manage to jab in my ticket and the machine cranked hungrily. It grabbed the ticket and almost sucked my fingers up the slot too. Although tears came to my eyes, which made it difficult to see whether blood had been drawn, I did not wince, nor flap my hand, nor stuff the pinched thumb into my mouth or under my arm. This took a great deal of self-control because of the pain and also because of the temptation to ham it up a bit, knowing I was the centre of attention. However, I resisted; I'm not a child; it was not my intention to give a public performance, I was merely endeavouring to fulfil my obligation to the bus company: a serious, legally correct enterprise.

There was a whirring noise, presumably the time/date/route were being stamped. When it stopped, I tried to withdraw the ticket - it wouldn't let go. I hammered the metal box a bit with my fist, first in the front, then on top. I could feel the smiles of satisfaction blooming on the faces of my audience.

Then a burly, blue-overalled chap from some archaeological/road-digging site gave the machine an almighty thump and the ticket came out into my hand with not a mark on it. I stared at it in disbelief and, just for a second, I was tempted to try again. The large digger-up of ancient ruins pursed his lips, shook his head and shrugged sadly. I deduced that the ink was dried up.

It was a let-down after all my effort. Some of my fellow passengers smiled at me sympathetically; they are so sympathetic, the Italians. I shrugged and smiled and tried to give away the rest of the little booklet of tickets I'd bought. They thought this a tremendous joke and shouted amusing quips, which I couldn't understand, as they got off the bus to stroll back to the bus-stop they should have got off at earlier.

# 7 Dry Season

Cindy woke in the night with a return of her nausea and stomach pains. Too many times in the past few weeks she'd huddled in the bathroom like this, waiting for them to ease. She watched the companion of her vigils, a snub-nosed gecko, scuttle across to where tiny flies danced around the naked light bulb, and she thought: 'Everything is food for something else. It's all killing and eating; eating and dying.'

Outside some heavy animal, a hippo, was moving on the lawn. Her ability to recognise animals from their sounds brought a certain satisfaction; she was an old hand now.

When they'd first arrived in the national game park every sound in the night, every whistle and squeak, had drawn her irresistibly to the window to try to discover which animal it was out there, living its secret life, so close and yet untouched by her existence. For them she was a shadow of no account; a cloud passing across the moon.

In her mind's eye she could see the great, barrel-bulk of the hippo, higher than the window sill, swinging its huge head from side to side as it tugged at the small green shoots, the only green shoots still around at this late stage in the dry season.

'The rains must come soon,' she murmured, not believing it.

Through the fine mesh screens, where mosquitoes fussed to get in, she could smell the sweet, acrid smoke of the grass fires that had been burning for days, both inside and outside the game park. The herdsmen liked to burn the old grass to stimulate the green shoots; a harsh treatment in a harsh land.

'How mankind everywhere thrashes and harries the earth, wrenching and chopping at it to make it bear fruit, constantly assaulting it!'

She felt salt tears on her lips.

'The wait's so long. All women weep in the dry season as though their tears provide an example for the rain.'

Suddenly a bushbuck whistled a warning from close at hand. Maybe there was a leopard about. She roused herself and wandered through the shadowy living room. The sky outside was pale; smoke-haze filtered the pre-dawn light. The lake lay like a dead thing with its humps of islands flat as cut-outs against the misty, cut-out hills. The mountain beyond them was long gone, lost, as though it had never existed anywhere except in the imagination.

Far away she heard a vehicle coming up the main track from the park entrance. It was probably the Rangers returning from an anti-poaching exercise. As it changed gear up the slope and entered the compound she realised it was not a Land Rover after all. Who could it be, coming into the Park at such an early hour? Tourists are forbidden to drive through the Park after dark because the outlines of animals dissolve in the night and they become one with its blackness.

The car turned towards the house. She heard its tyres crunch to a halt at the back. A car door flapped shut. Soon someone was knocking and calling at her servant's house and she guessed who it must be.

There was a scuffling with the key, the kitchen door was flung open, and there was her cook struggling with a huge bag of vegetables. They'd actually remembered to bring food with them - what a relief.

Then George came in, big and tall, his white smile preceded him through the gloom. He was talking as always, but quietly, as he suggested and countermanded his own suggestions. Had he come alone? No. A small boy stole in, half asleep. Then, because he could see Cindy watching them like a ghost from the living room, he wound an arm round his father's leg.

She forced herself onto the scene, switching on the light and greeting George with a long handshake and, "How good to see you. It's such a long time since you were last here."

She touched the tight curls of the beautiful child, and bent to ask his name - and oh, the brilliant smile, and dark, liquid eyes, enormous, enormous in the chubby, chocolate baby face. How she wanted to kiss and cuddle him, and wanted him to put his little arms around her.

She found her flipflop sandals and went out to the car to help Myrtle with the other children.

"We've all been asleep," laughed Myrtle, hugging Cindy with the arm that was not holding the baby.

"We would have been quite happy to stay in the car until everyone woke up, but you know what George is like." She was embarrassed by her husband's lack of courtesy. "Such an unsociable hour to arrive; waking you up, Cindy, it's disgraceful."

"No, no, I was awake. I always wake up early. Graham's still asleep, of course. I'll go and get him."

"You do no such thing. It was no good trying to warn you we were coming: the post is so slow."

Cindy was puzzled. Why had they decided to set out from the capital so late in the day? It was cooler, of course, but far more dangerous with unlit lorries left on the road, suicidal animals wandering about without even reflectors on their backsides and then there were the bandits that reputedly blocked the road on lonely stretches.

"Was the road bad?" she asked, thinking perhaps they'd started early and been delayed by miles of greasy mud. When a lorry gets bogged down in mud, traffic can be held up for hours or even days. Then she remembered that it had not rained for weeks.

The bundles and boxes were brought in. George was his usual ebullient self. He'd brought a crate of beer for Graham. Myrtle seemed harassed and tired. In the rush, several things she needed for the baby had been left behind.

Jessica, the eldest, mothered her mother, bringing her a glass of water as she sat on the edge of Cindy's sofa with the baby clamped to a productive teat.

Cindy said: "You and George, and the baby, can use the guest house, if you like. Jessica and the boys will be all right in the spare room here, won't they?"

Myrtle looked round for her husband who was in the kitchen telling the cook about the meat he'd brought.

Cindy could hear the cook grunting acknowledgements. She wondered if he was pleased to see George again. He had been his cook when George used to live in the house next door - that was before he married. Jessica must be eight now. There had been four children since, including the tiny baby sucking so strongly and peacefully.

Cindy went over to the window. She wanted them all to go away. She did not want Myrtle and her baby and all her children staying with her in her house.

The sun was up now, and the lake shone like a mirror. The hippo were honking and splashing down in the shallow inlet at the foot of the long slope below the house. Hidden in the long grass, or among the bushes or in burrows or hollow trees, all the mother animals were suckling their young - or they would be soon, as soon as the rains came. All the wombs in the world were waiting, ready for the first splattering drops of rain.

She thought she heard a fisherman pounding the water with his oar to scare the fish into his net.

'Good,' she thought, 'there'll be fish for lunch.' Then she wondered if she'd imagined it because it seemed unlikely that any fisherman would venture far onto the lake in such poor visibility. With a shock, she noticed that the opposite shore of their bay, including all the little white houses of the fishing village, had gone. Like the great mountain, it was as though they'd never existed. The edge of reality had crept a little nearer, her world was shrinking fast.

"It's the school holidays and since I'm still on maternity leave, George wanted to bring the children to see the animals," Myrtle explained.

'I wonder,' mused Cindy, 'do they expect Graham and I to move into the guest house? Is Myrtle insulted because I suggested their staying there instead of here? It's very small, only a bedroom and bathroom. Why doesn't she say something?'

Cindy went to shake Graham. He woke, thinking that it was an earth tremor,

"The Park's very dry," commented George, after breakfast. "I've never seen it so dry."

"You must have forgotten," Cindy teased. "It's always like this."

"I'd thought of taking the kids to the Craters, but it's a bit hazy," said George.

He went off with Graham to discuss conservation matters.

Myrtle and Cindy watched the children playing. They were collecting items to make a 'museum': the sloughed skin of a snake, a weaver bird's nest, feathers, pieces of quartz and a dead chick.

"Did you kill it?" Myrtle demanded suspiciously, but ants had already eaten its eyes so the children were innocent.

"Leave it, leave it where it was," shouted Tom, bullying his brother and sister. "The ants will finish cleaning it and then we can take back the skeleton."

'I like Myrtle,' Cindy decided. 'She's been such a good friend. She invites us to stay with her every time we have to go up to the capital. The least I can do in return is to put her up for a few days. What else would I be doing? Pretending to help Graham? No, I'm delighted she's come.'

It was a lie. She wanted them to leave before they were all trapped together, shut in by the wall of steadily thickening, smoke-laden air.

'It's George,' she thought, 'I can't stand George. He's always so full of himself. Perhaps he senses my disapproval and that's why he shows off and scores points all the time. Poor Myrtle.'

That was a falsehood too. Myrtle was not poor. Myrtle never did anything she did not want to do. Back in town Cindy had often heard her employing such a range of subtle and inventive wiles, it made your head spin.

No, it was not because of some rumoured military coup that they'd left the capital in such a rush. It was because Myrtle wanted to get away and had issued an ultimatum. Cindy could picture George rushing round to the local market buying up huge quantities of fruit and vegetables, with his gardener in tow to carry them back to the car.

They hadn't brought the nursemaid with them. Presumably Jessica was considered old enough to keep an eye on the younger ones.

"Myrtle, just look where they've got to," cried Cindy. "It's dangerous for them to be off down the slope like that.

There could be all kinds of animals in that gully," Myrtle yelled at Jessica, "snakes at least."

"Don't worry, it's quite safe, Mummy. Come and see what we've found."

Gingerly Cindy and Myrtle picked their way over the dried up, prickly weeds that covered the bare slope and stood looking down into the gully where bushes shimmered, their leaves wilting in the heat.

"Well, they've been making such a racket they've scared away all the game," laughed Myrtle.

The women admired the 'museum' finds: bent metal cooking pots, broken saucers, half a plastic lavatory seat (which was causing a great argument), some buggy wheels too rusty to be useful, and the prize: a gramophone record not even scratched.

"This must be where they threw all the rubbish when they pulled down George's old house," said Cindy. "Look, those are the roof beams and the thatch. The termites had eaten most of the walls even before they were taken down. But, Myrtle, there must be snakes under all that."

Myrtle called off her brood: "I think you've found all the interesting things now. The rest's only rubbish." She winked at Cindy. "Now you can come and sit in the shade on the veranda and write the labels for everything. You're so hot." She wiped the little one's sweaty face.

They began to climb back up the slope, all except Tom.

"Hey, just look at this." His voice was full of wonder. He was pulling what looked like a paling out from the old reed thatch. "This is just what we need for our museum. Wow! What animal did this come from, Mummy?"

Cindy and Myrtle turned back to examine Tom's find. The other children had gathered round and were stroking the long, thin bone with suitable appreciation.

"I think it might be from a dinosaur," speculated Tom.

"No. It's a buffalo," said Myrtle, in a flash. She looked up at Cindy and saw that she too had recognised that it was unmistakably a human thigh bone. It could be nothing else.

"I'm practically certain it's a dinosaur," said Tom.

"Well, if it is, you won't be able to keep it, will you?" replied his mother. "It'll be too archaeologically important. Put it with the other things."

She shook her head so Cindy would make no comment about the bone. When they were alone she whispered: "They'll have forgotten about it by tomorrow."

"But the police will have to be informed," cried Cindy, horrified that a human bone should become a child's plaything. "It could be from a murder victim."

"They won't be able to tell much from half a leg," laughed Myrtle. "She died in the park so the hyaenas and vultures will have scattered the bones."

"They might find the skull. Why did you say 'she'?"

"These barmaids, poor things, they come and go. Nobody bothers much if a girl disappears."

"But murdered in front of my house ...."

"What makes you think it was murder? She was probably drunk and blundered into a buffalo. It has been known. Anyway, it happened years ago. That bone's very old."

The children were trying to polish the pale bone with sand and handfuls of dry leaves. Cindy looked up. Even the islands in the lake had disintegrated.

The glassy water stretched away into an infinity of nothingness. Suddenly the cramps gripped her stomach again and she rushed to the bathroom. Behind the closed door she could think.

Myrtle was right. What could the police do in this country where death was everyone's bedfellow?

She thought about the poor girl, lost in the Park with no one to miss or mourn her. Then it came to Cindy with great certainty that she had seen the woman, long ago, back in those innocent, green days, when they'd first arrived. She'd seen her visiting the thatched, palm-log cottage where George had lived before his marriage. She'd heard the girl screaming in the night; heard her weeping, begging George not to leave her but to take her back to the city with him. She'd felt the girl's heart breaking as if it had been her own - crying out, calling in the night.

"Are you all right, Cindy?" Myrtle was anxiously tapping on the door.

Cindy came out. She was shaking with terror. She knew. She could see it clearly.

"No, I'm ill. I must get away from here."

Myrtle was shocked at her appearance. She held her hand as she listened sympathetically to the symptoms.

"So you see, he's poisoning me," Cindy finished up.

"What are you talking about? Who's poisoning you?" Myrtle scoffed at the very idea of gentle Graham's doing anything of the sort.

When the men returned for lunch, Cindy was almost packed.

Graham came to her.

"It was the bone, Darling. I know that's what's upset you. Just calm down. Forget about it, Darling. This is Africa, after all."

"George killed her," she breathed.

"Don't talk such rot."

"Now you're trying to get rid of me." The tears fell so easily.

"Oh dear," he sighed wearily, "Not again. This is all about our not having any children, isn't it? I've told you a thousand times, I'm perfectly happy as we are. I don't blame you. Who knows, it may be my fault."

She screamed once and the look of hatred on her face frightened him. She hit away his arms as he reached to comfort her.

"I'm going now, today, before I'm swallowed up in the fog," she said firmly.

She glanced out, even the lake had disappeared.

"But you can't. You've got guests. Pull yourself together. What are people going to think? Just calm down. In a day or two, when the rains come, you'll be all right."

"No, I won't."

She didn't wait to eat. The thick smoky air was already creeping up the slope. She put her suitcase in the car. As she drove out through the compound gate, she thought she heard a distant roll of thunder.

When she reached the top of the hill marking the boundary of the park, she stopped to gaze back across the murk-filled valley. There on the opposite side was the great mountain; it had returned; its peaks were enveloped in dark cloud; grey curtains of rain were streaming down onto its lower slopes.

Cindy lifted her head and breathed deeply. Drifting towards her on the breeze, was the sweet, fertile promise of the rains.

It was over. She was free. The relief made her smile. At which, her ugly stomach pain turned away its crooked head, gathered itself up and took to the air. She watched it flapping its heavy wings as it made its way, back into the park.

# 8  Old Enemies

When I met Samantha and Vanessa again after a gap of more than thirty years, I honestly didn't recognise them, not at first, not for quite some time.

During their school days, like most girls growing up, they both altered quite a bit, Vanessa especially: she changed from an ugly duckling into a swan. Even so, for them both to have gone to such lengths to achieve such a complete make-over; almost a disguise. Well, all I can say is: there's hope for us all.

Back then at school, gorgeous Sam and admirable Vanessa only bothered with podgy little me because I had this rather dishy-looking elder brother.

Everyone in town knew who Guy was. On a Saturday morning, you could stand at the top of our high street and tell at a glance where he was from the knot of youngsters, mostly female, round him. I went along once, just to see what the great draw was - I mean, those idiotic girls would be hanging about half the morning, unless the police moved them on. I found the whole thing dead boring: a few really feeble jokes and long periods of nothing, except of course, for the spectacle of Guy, propping up a lamppost, looking pale and interesting. He used to get my poor mother to press his trousers before he went out. (Being a mere girl, I had to iron my own clothes. How things have changed - one hopes.) He'd tuck a silk cravat into a newish-looking shirt. (He must have been given a lot more pocket-money than I ever got.) What really set the girls drooling in those days was the long tongue of auburn hair licking his left eyebrow.

In the Sam/Guy/Vanessa happening back then, I'd had my own agenda: first of all, I desperately wanted to be picked for the school hockey team. I used to practise dribbling the ball round the garden, and then I'd slam it into a goal drawn on the garage wall. Hours I used to spend, rushing about in hockey boots, flicking away with the stick, but whether I was inspired by love of the game or by love of tall, lithesome Samantha, I'm now not so sure. Those were innocent times. We'd never heard of gays or lesbians. Half the girls in school, those that weren't mooning after my bad brother, had 'crushes' on their teachers.

When accused, I always strenuously denied that I had a 'crush' on Sam. It was control over the hockey ball I thought I wanted, not control over the hockey captain. However, one day I overheard Sam making some remark about Guy – I seized the moment and intercepted her in the bike sheds.

"Come to my birthday pyjama party next Saturday," I said, guaranteeing a close encounter with Guy. I was convinced that if my brother were to become her boyfriend, she'd jolly well have to pick me for the hockey team, even though I was a year below her.

Naturally our 'Joan Hunter-Dunn of the hockey pitch' accepted my invitation. At the end of the party, when fathers in cars were arriving to pick up their daughters, Guy dropped by to cast a predatory eye over my friends, as I knew he would - even though he said they were all too young.

Guy was hooked at once. Samantha stood head and shoulders above the crowd. Not only that, there was a natural grace about the way she did everything. Guy offered her a cigarette, - part of the mating ritual in the days before we knew about cancer. Their eyes met over the flickering flame from his lighter but Samantha seemed strangely unimpressed by the flick of auburn hair and earnest grey-green eyes. Like a Hollywood starlet, she blew out a cloud of cigarette smoke and drooped back the wrist of her cigarette hand, (she must have been practising in front of the mirror). She thanked him, with only the slightest suggestion of a smile, and then she deliberately turned her back on him. Clever girl. Not only was she brilliant at sport, with a model's face and figure, she also had brains enough to intrigue Guy.

The real high-flyer in the brains department, however, was Vanessa, our deputy head girl. She started off looking the typical ultra-studious type: lank mousey hair, and bottle-end glasses. But suddenly she started shaving her legs and we guessed she was beginning to take an interest in her appearance - if not in boys.

By this time, Guy and Sam were 'going steady' and I was blissfully happy in the hockey team. Looking back, I can see that I ought not to have pushed my luck for a second time, but I'd caught the whiff of power, and couldn't resist playing my trump card again.

My hockey triumphs had brought me a certain prestige among the sporty girls, but I craved to be noticed by the swots-set as well. To do this, I planned to gain a place on our highly successful Debating Team where Vanessa was its star captain. My problem was how to get Guy to take an interest in a dowdy little Vanessa. Then I had a brilliant idea.

"Sam," I said, bursting into the front sitting room one Friday evening as soon as I saw Guy pop upstairs to the loo.

Samantha began tugging down her skirt and adjusting her blouse. Obviously, some heavy petting had been going on. If my parents had left me in the house to act as chaperon while they went to meet friends, then I'd obviously fallen down on the job.

"Sam, don't you think Vanessa would make the perfect Juliet? You know, Romeo and Juliet? The school play? She's got such a brilliant voice. She's a born actress."

Here I sighed. "Only she always looks such a mess nobody's going to consider her for the part. Of course, you're the only possible choice for Romeo." (In girls' schools the male roles have to be played by girls, of course.)

I stared hard at the toe of her nylons dangling out from under a cushion. Why would she undo her suspenders unless it was to get her panties off? Samantha actually blushed. After that, she was putty in my hands.

At my bidding, Samantha took control of Vanessa's appearance. She permed and tinted her hair and persuaded her to leave off her glasses. (Without them, her eyes were like deep blue velvet.) What's more, Sam somehow managed to transform Vanessa's sack-of-potatoes figure into something bordering on normal. (Maybe her mother had never let her buy a bra before.) It was all worth it: Vanessa got the part of Juliet opposite Samantha's Romeo.

Guy went to the school play to admire Sam in her Romeo-tights but all through rehearsals, I'd been feeding him propaganda about Vanessa. I told my mother, in his hearing, how simply marvellous Vanessa was as Juliet; how she could charm a bird out of a tree with the beauty of her voice; how she'd won the East of England Debating Cup; how she'd been accepted at Oxford University and how a famous film producer had come to the first night of the play and there was a rumour that he'd offered her a contract to work in Hollywood and how she was torn between an academic career and fame and fortune ... etc etc. (The film producer was a lie - I tend to get carried away.)

The result was, when Guy saw Vanessa on stage, (she really did look stunning with all the make-up and lighting etc) he decided that she should be his next girlfriend. He was probably getting bored with poor Sam, as men did in those days, 'once they'd had their way with you.'

The local paper printed a glowing review of Vanessa's performance, plus a flattering photo. Vanessa would indeed make a good catch for Guy, but getting her to take him seriously proved a tough nut to crack. Guy would never have persevered if I hadn't assured him that, despite her apparent reluctance, Vanessa was totally smitten. At the same time, I happened to mention to my mother, pretending I didn't know Guy was around, that Samantha had been seen kissing another boy.

Although everyone knew Guy was chasing Vanessa, he continued to see Sam. (Guy couldn't possibly be girlfriendless.) It was obvious, however, that their ardour had cooled. Quarrelling could frequently be heard, and sad to say, the late nights or the weeping after the rows were taking their toll on our gorgeous hockey captain. She'd lost her sparkle and much of her speed on the hockey field.

"Guy, if you're serious about Vanessa," I advised, "why don't you join your school debating society?"

It worked. She noticed him. To get her to himself, however, he had to pretend a great anxiety about attaining good grades in his exams. He actually wrote bits of essays so that Vanessa would help him finish them. Naturally my parents were delighted by this unexpected turn-around in his work-ethic; they encouraged Guy's friendship with Vanessa for all they were worth.

Poor Sam took the break-up pretty badly; we lost six-nil in the last match she played in, just before she started limping and was dropped from the team. I didn't fret too much over the demoralized state of school hockey because I'd been given my chance with the Debating Soc. I was beginning to think Vanessa would make an ideal sister-in-law when I began to notice that some of the girls at school were whispering and giving me really odd looks.

Somebody said to me: "Sam's putting on weight, isn't she?" but the penny didn't drop.

Suddenly everyone was taking sides. My former chums in the hockey team sided with Sam against Vanessa and me. I couldn't work out what was going on. Then there was a terrific upset at home. My mother had hysterics. I heard her shouting that I must never be told the truth because it would ruin my life as well as Guy's.

I went straight to Guy to find out what was going on. He looked a bit wobbly round the gills. His bright hair had lost its bounce and flopped right down to the end of his nose.

"That stupid Samantha's got herself pregnant and she says it's mine. What was the name of that other boy you said she was seeing?"

I was shocked. I felt guilty because it was partly my fault. I had introduced them.

Samantha got fatter and fatter and then she disappeared from school. When she came back the following year, we were told she'd been in a T.B. sanatorium. Anyone less like a T.B. sufferer you could hardly imagine - she'd put on so much weight. People were so hypocritical in those days, I mean, everyone knew she'd had Guy's baby. And the way some of the girls treated me – like I had some infectious disease or something! I went around telling my erstwhile friends that I'd tried to persuade my mother to adopt the baby - which wasn't true - the subject could never be mentioned in our house.

Guy was sent away to boarding school to be 'kept under stricter control'. From what he told me in the holidays about the trainee junior-school matron, I doubt that was the case.

Samantha had become a totally different person. She'd cut off her lovely, thick plaits and wore her gymslip really long to cover up her fat thighs. She never did anything - no hockey, no tennis, nothing except try to catch up on her studies. The science teacher took her under her wing and gave her extra tuition. She'd walk away if she saw me coming, but I used to hear her laughing raucously with girls she'd never bothered with before. Her laugh had changed. Actually, I don't remember her ever laughing when she was hockey captain - hockey was much too serious.

Vanessa, strangely, seemed even more affected by the whole business. She went completely to pieces and never got her scholarship to Oxford. She latched onto me whenever she saw me, and repeatedly told me how she would love Guy till the end of time and such-like twaddle. I guess she'd never had a boyfriend before. She would also go on about how she'd never forgive Samantha for what she'd done to Guy.

"What do you mean?"

"I mean, getting herself pregnant on purpose so that he'd have to marry her."

We had this conversation so many times and finally I gave up trying to get her to see sense.

"Now he's terrified of girls. That's why he won't speak to me anymore. That scheming Samantha, she's ruined his life and mine."

Then she'd cry a bit.

In fact, Guy's being sent away to school was the best thing that could have happened from the point of view of his studies and future career – no more loitering around town on a Saturday morning.

I considered telling Vanessa about the junior-school matron and how Guy was bad news as far as women were concerned, but sisterly loyalty made me hold my tongue. I don't suppose it would have lessened her devotion to Guy, anyway.

Then last year, just before my fiftieth birthday, our paths crossed again.

I'd managed to wangle a job as a tour-guide shepherding groups of international tourists round some of the best Nature Reserves and National Parks in the United States. These two middle-aged women were part of a very mixed bunch. Both had different surnames so I presume they'd both married, although neither was with a partner. They weren't together so I guess they didn't recognise each other, not at first, and I certainly wouldn't have recognised either of them. As I mentioned earlier, they might almost have assumed disguises.

However, when I was checking my group onto the coach one day, Samantha made herself known to me. "You look just like your dear mother," she said, which rather grated, and almost set us off on the wrong foot. However, she bore no grudge, as far as I could tell, and wanted to be friendly - wanted to know about Guy, of course.

I would have said at that point that having Guy's baby and putting it up for adoption had left no scars, but you can never be quite sure. Samantha had become very willowy again, almost frail. In fact she was so thin, her face seemed quite altered. Her now-blond hair was cut very short but the main difference was her voice. I would never have recognised it. It was so gravelly, (too much smoking, probably) with an arty, high-class affectation you could cut with a knife. She'd obviously done very well for herself, financially at least.

I find it hard to believe that Vanessa didn't recognise me. After all, I was using my own name and I was still dumpy with the same frizzy hair-do, so she obviously didn't want me to know who she was. She was calling herself 'Nessa Chang', her hair was now black and she'd had a nose-job: in place of the normal large English hooter she had an oriental-type button. Heavy mascara disguised her blue eyes, now equipped with contact lenses. Then there was the way she walked and dressed and the neat little gestures with her hands. I'd never noticed before how small they were. I assumed she was half Chinese. She hardly said anything, just nodded and smiled, but on the odd occasion when I did hear her speaking, her voice seemed high-pitched and feminine, quite unlike her old confident, beautifully modulated debater's voice. I certainly didn't recognise it.

At some point during the tour Vanessa must have recognised Samantha, and she began to strike up a friendship with her. Sam can't have known who Nessa Chang really was, or she would have told me. Or would she?

In Yosemite National Park, which was the last stop on the tour, there is a place where a flat rock juts out over a narrow valley that some ancient glacier once carved through the mountains. The drop must be at least a hundred metres. It's undoubtedly one of the most spectacular views anywhere in the world.

Unfortunately, in the guidebook there's a photograph of some idiots, not just standing on this jutting rock, but apparently performing a dance. There's also a picture of Teddy Roosevelt standing on it, admiring the scenery. Today, of course, there's a barrier to discourage people from getting out onto this dangerous platform. You can imagine my horror when I saw two of my party clambering over the fence. They'd handed their cameras to another idiot to take photos of them.

Suddenly, just as I heard Samantha's old raucous laugh, I caught sight of the expression on Vanessa's face and I knew immediately, without the shadow of a doubt, who she was. The shock of recognition almost floored me - my mind flew to envisaging an impending disaster. What on earth were they doing out there, those two school arch-rivals, circling round, gripping each other's biceps? They were dancing, or at least, kicking their legs in the air. Were they both drunk? Sam couldn't possibly have recognised that it was Vanessa to whom she was entrusting her life. Poor Samantha, my hockey captain heroine!

"Come back in, come back in at once," I shouted in my best school-marm voice, as soon as I'd got enough spittle in my mouth. I gazed desperately about for a park official. I could feel my pulse-rate rocketing.

Alternatively, perhaps Sam had recognised Vanessa but had not revealed her own identity. Perhaps it was Sam, not Vanessa, who was planning some terrible revenge.

I wanted to warn them both but my voice wouldn't come. My knees buckled. I was shaking so much I collapsed in a heap just after I'd clambered over the fence to join them. I couldn't catch my breath. I thought I was going to have a heart attack.

It was my intention to grab Samantha's ankles as I lay flat on the rock. I trusted that my considerable weight would be enough to stop us both toppling to our death. But suppose it was Samantha, after all, who was about to chuck Vanessa down into the abyss? I should grab her ankle too.

I crawled forward, very slowly, with arm out-stretched. If they both fell, I would almost certainly be dragged over the precipice too. Better that, I decided, than live forever with the guilt. I squirmed forward another two inches.

Behind me cameras were clicking. Our collective demise would be well documented. My grasping fingers were still out of range of the ankles and I hadn't even reached the part where the rock stuck out over the void.

"Sam, Sam," I choked and spluttered. "Be careful, please!"

Time was running out but there was no way I could have stood up. I could hear them both laughing. Were they laughing at me; laughing together and dancing, one tall, one short, urging me to join them? Was I going to be the object of their joint revenge? Had they been planning this all along?

I must have passed out then.

Afterwards, that evening, they came and bought me a drink at the bar and apologised.

"If it had been Guy instead of you, we might have thrown him over," laughed Samantha.

"But possibly not," said Vanessa in her new small voice.

After a while I relaxed a little. Could we be old school friends together, simply reminiscing about old times? No, my feelings of guilt ran far too deep for that.

# 9  Driving to Places in East Africa

Every week or so, one or two of us would cross the Equator to shop for food in the Northern Hemisphere. If supplied with lists and cash, we'd shop for the other biologists, who were carrying out research in one of the most beautiful and scenically varied National Park in East Africa.

It was a long drive over dirt roads to the foothills of the Mountains of the Moon, where the copper mining town of Kilembe once boasted a supermarket that stocked exotic items like packets of cornflakes, Heinz mayonnaise and luxury shampoos.

After the supermarket closed, the drive was a few miles shorter, but we'd always shopped in the local market in Kasese for our fruit and vegetables anyway. The market was always far more interesting, with wooden animal carvings or bead work or colourful woven grass mats and a variety of wonderful baskets to admire as well as the chance of maybe finding a different vegetable. Matoke, the green bananas that could be mashed like potatoes, was always available, and onions, tomatoes, Irish potatoes and the big white drum cabbages but if there happened to be carrots or the rarely grown leeks or best of all, the wild spinach, we were thrilled. Avocadoes were very cheap but seasonal, of course. Sometimes there were sweet potatoes and dry cobs of maize. There were always peanuts, small sweet bananas, pawpaw and bitter oranges and usually you'd find someone selling the most delicious pineapples. That was it. To buy mangos, peppers, or cauliflowers, you had to travel twice the distance to the big market in Fort Portal, the local administrative centre.

Once, taking many shopping bags, I accompanied my husband who was going there to pay some taxes. It was an eighty miles drive, some of it on tarmac, which was a great luxury after bumping over the hard, corrugated surface of a dirt road in the dry season - always in a cloud of dust. If another vehicle was approaching down the centre of the road in another cloud of dust, you indicated this to any following vehicle with your turn-right light.

We had not long left the rough road through the Park and were sailing along so smoothly over a fairly new tarmac road when I suddenly noticed, running alongside us and trying to overtake us up the slight incline, a smallish wheel. Were children around, playing with an old tyre? No. There was no one else to be seen and certainly no other vehicle. The explanation must be that the wheel belonged to us and the car we were driving had only three wheels. We slowed to a halt beside the road and then my husband got out and chased after the spinning wheel for many metres along the road. I remained in the car to keep it level until he'd place the jack under the car and slipped on the escaped wheel.

I was most surprised that all that juddering could loosen the nuts holding on the wheel; usually they're tightened really well by the strong, cheery mechanics in the Park's workshop. I knew this because of what had happened a few weeks earlier when I'd driven to the Kasese market with my two small children - no one else had wanted to come - the three shopping lists weren't excessively long so we were returning in good time when halfway home we had a puncture.

Punctures are not a rare occurrence where the thorns on trees and bushes are long, strong and sharp. The heat of the midday sun might also weaken previous repairs and the roads are full of sharp stones that are flung up constantly as you drive along. They hit the floor of the vehicle creating an alarming noise, and that, together with the constant rattle of every part of the metal Land Rover, means all communication is made by shouting.

The wonky steering showed that one tyre was flat so I slowed to a stop near where some tall eucalyptus grew not far from the road. I thought maybe the children could stand in the shade while I changed the wheel – the noon sun was directly overhead. However, this didn't turn out to be such a good idea because, whilst collecting small rocks to wedge under the wheels, I noticed some very fresh pug marks in the sand at the roadside. At least two lionesses had crossed the road and passed that way fairly recently. Possibly they too had decided to rest in the shade of the eucalyptus trees. Were they watching us or were they asleep? The shrill voices of small children might have aroused their interest but my kids were half asleep, exhausted by the heat and by trying to help with the heavy shopping bags.

"Stay close to the Land Rover." There was a sliver of shade beside the scorching metal box. "Keep a look out and tell me if you see any animals." I'd shown them the foot prints and together we'd decided that they were too big to be those of a leopard.

Most animals rest in the heat of the day. I looked around. Nothing moved: no warthog family was scampering between the thorn bushes. Only the cicadas in the dense eucalyptus kept up a continuous, near-deafening racket. The northern swampy fringes of the lake lay a few miles away, beyond the scattered tangles of thorny vegetation, each of which protected a cactus-like *euphoria candelabra* tree from the rampages of hungry elephants. The lions had probably crossed the road to drink from the lake and perhaps they'd returned to protect a recent kill. I sniffed the air and detected no whiff of rotting corpse but then I spotted a few vultures perched in an acacia tree less than half a mile away.

"Keep close and if you see a lion, jump inside," I told my little children as I set up the jack and lifted out the spare wheel which seemed to be inflated and fit to go. I found the large wheel-brace and fitted it onto the nuts that attached the wheel with its punctured tyre. I pulled and pushed. I readjusted and stood on the brace. I even attempted a risky jump, but there was no way I could budge any of the well-tightened nuts. We were stuck there under the equatorial sun waiting to be rescued by some passing strongman – this was long before mobile phones were invented.

Sooner or later a truck would come by, we just had to be patient. Someone would come looking for us when we didn't get home. We had water and plenty of bananas to eat and there was a story book we could read. The Land Rover continued to absorb heat even though all the doors and the bonnet were open. Then a slight breeze came creeping towards us from the lake so, even though we had no shade, we felt a little cooler. The trouble was the breeze would carry our scent towards the lionesses hidden somewhere over there. But they wouldn't be hungry if they had a kill, nor would they like the smell of the vehicle.

We waited, sitting on the sandy gravel, alert and listening - just in case. Then, after less than an hour, we heard a pickup truck approaching and jumped up joyfully to wave.

The driver and his passenger were out of the truck and they'd changed the wheel as swiftly as a team in a motor race. I thanked them profusely and showed them the lion footprints. This made the event even more amusing for them. At least they had a good story to tell their friends in the bar that evening, about a pathetically weak woman who was afraid of lions.

I don't know why we didn't fly to the meeting of conservationists in the Serengeti – maybe the Cessna was undergoing its major annual service in Nairobi. Instead we had to drive in the only available vehicle: the minibus. Hardly had we left the Park before we realised there was a problem: the minibus was leaking oil faster than it was using petrol. Filling up with oil at every garage on route made us late getting to Kampala where we eventually swapped the minibus for a hired Land Rover. Then it was a race to get across the border before it closed for the night. We found a motel just as it got dark but I seem to remember we couldn't find anywhere to eat. I think we ate our emergency biscuits before we fell asleep.

In the morning we bought food for the journey and set off in plenty of time to reach our destination inside the Serengeti National Park. We were ahead of schedule, there should have been no problem.

Bouncing along the dirt road in a cloud of dust in the middle of nowhere we had our first puncture. No problem – except that when we examined the spare wheel properly, we discovered that it would never have passed an MOT - had such a thing existed then. It came as no surprise therefore, when a few miles further on the spare went flat: our second puncture. It wasn't far to the next small town so my husband decided to drive slowly on the worn-out flat spare. "It's finished anyway. We'll try to buy another spare."

Of course, in that isolated spot, there was no new or second-hand tyre to fit our wheel but the cheery mechanic, after he'd repaired the first puncture, worked away at a tyre he'd found and made it fit the spare wheel so that we would have something to drive on if we had another puncture. It was late by that time so we stayed the night there and set off early the next morning.

We passed through the gate into the Park and I saw my first wild giraffes, so big they seemed to be running away in slow motion. We passed a few buffalo and groups of antelope. Then, many miles short of our destination, we had two more punctures in quick succession. We tottered along slowly on a flat tyre as far as a Park Ranger's post, set beneath the wide-spreading branches of some fever trees growing near a small watercourse.

The Ranger assured us there'd be another vehicle along soon, and sure enough, after a couple of hours, along came a pickup truck, which kindly stopped to help. The driver was happy to take my husband, plus punctured wheel, on board because there was just enough room for him to squeeze in between a Masai herdsman in his red blanket clutching a spear and a traditionally bead-bedecked woman breast-feeding her baby.

I waved him off and went to chat to the Ranger who seemed pleased to have someone to practise his English with. He told me it was a lonely life but he introduced me to his best friend who kept him company: a spry, long-legged rooster. "We do exercises together like this." The man and the rooster ran around in circles, but who was chasing whom, I could not say for sure.

Communication was a bit of a struggle, what with his limited English and my even poorer grasp of Swahili. The afternoon drew on; he told me that some evenings a rhino came to drink from the small river hidden close-by among the yellow scrub of acacia saplings. Even in those days, rhinos were rare and I was quite keen to see one. "Is it dangerous for you to go outside at night?" I asked. He shook his head. "The animals do not come close," he said. It was his supper time; he ate some maize kernels that he'd softened in a tin-can over the fire. He offered me a coffee in his only mug. I didn't think to ask him if the rooster stayed the night in his room but thinking about it now, I guess it was probably the safest place for it. So many animals would like to eat a rooster. "What about leopards?" "Oh yes, a leopard lives near here."

Night falls early in the tropics and it was getting dark when we heard the pickup truck returning. The Ranger brought a lantern and helped my husband to change the wheel. Then an almost full moon came up, so driving through the park was not quite as hazardous as it might have been.

They had been expecting us at the Safari Lodge and so, before he went off-duty, the cook had made sandwiches for us to eat in our tent before, half-asleep already, we fell into our camp beds.

I don't recall that we had any punctures during the return journey. Maybe the mechanics in the workshop did a good re-sticking job on all the previous patches, or maybe they swapped some of the wheels from other Land Rovers.

# 10  The Babel Factor

The Education Inspector was to visit our English class for immigrants, so although the weather was bad, attendance was good. Even Mrs Shah, wearing her best sari in honour of the Inspector, was only twenty minutes late. Her feet, in gold-thonged sandals, did not appear to be suffering from frost bite, despite the sleet, which dashed against the classroom windows.

After greetings and an exchange of news, followed by a short 'grammar session' using the whiteboard, we went into the coffee-room for a well-earned break. This was always followed by the 'conversation class' when our students, mostly immigrant wives, practised 'useful' phrases for 'everyday situations': 'Please could you tell me the way to the post office?' or 'How much is that (*insert your own item*) in the window?' Sometimes our role-play acting was a little bit more ambitious: 'Parents' evening at school' or 'At the doctor's surgery.'

I didn't actually see our lady Inspector, Barbara Edwards, drop her empty coffee mug. Before she sank gracefully to the floor, they tell me that she'd called out dramatically: "Poison! Fetch a doctor!"

This was because at the time, I was scowling bad-temperedly through the serving hatch into the kitchen, where Natasha was helping the ever-smiling

Fumi to wash up our coffee cups. It wasn't Natasha's turn to make the coffee and wash up but she'd only just arrived - I'd been fervently hoping she'd forget to come but I knew things never get that lucky.

Only when Natasha approached the hatch and looked over my shoulder and yelled in her deep, penetrating voice: "My Got. Bloodyell. What she do?" did I turn and see everyone gathered around the prostrate body of the education officer. The more fluent students were repeating useful phrases like: 'Is she breathing?' 'Can you feel a pulse?' 'Call an ambulance.' 'Call the police.'

"Hey!" Natasha shouted through the hatch. "Hey, what mean this: 'po lease'? In dictionary it say: 'po' mean 'under-bed potty' for, how you call it, wee-wee?" Her black eyes glittered with glee. Her scarlet lips revealed the studs of gold in her large teeth as she smiled at me. I sighed and shook my head at her.

"Sorry Teacher. I must not learn the others THE very bad words. Sorry, my English no good." Then she called loudly: "I sorry every body, scrub that."

"Wait there in the kitchen," I hissed at Natasha.

First I checked that Jenny, the volunteer who taught the Beginners, was coping. During the class last week she'd felt unwell and had left early. She still looked washed out. Dark rings circled her eyes, but she was busy in the far corner teaching her group how to make an emergency phone call. On the small whiteboard she wrote: 'Emergency', 'service', 'fire', 'police' and 'ambulance' and had them all repeating the words, so I left her to it and went to tackle Natasha who wouldn't remain in the kitchen for long.

At some time or another, every adult foreign language class experiences the constant interruptions of some prima donna who wants to hold centre stage. Natasha had only been coming to the class since the summer though she'd been living in England for some time. She had a teenage daughter attending the local school and from her she picked up many idiomatic expressions. She could usually make herself understood but she still couldn't put three words together correctly. The other students were picking up her lack of grammar and poor pronunciation, and even some of her bad language. I thought of locking her in the kitchen but she'd only crawl out through the hatch causing maximum disruption.

Her expensive perfume was approaching down the passage and I waited to grab her. Her formidable biceps felt hard beneath the softness of her cashmere sweater. "Have you finished helping Fumi?" I asked her.

"Is no my turn. Fumi O.K" She shrugged me off. "Now I come to help for this murdering."

"Listen, Natasha please be good. The school inspector agreed to help with this role-play. Please let the others speak. Let them answer the questions we practised last week. You understand? Please be quiet."

"Shurrup, you mean?"

I nodded.

"Why you no say 'shurrup', then? I know why today you say: 'Natasha shurrup! Hold your trap', is becoss Mrs Barbara THE school inspector! O.K. I understand. I carn speak good my English. O.K. Is alright. I shurrup. I good girl today."

I imagined that Natasha had never in her life been what is generally considered to be 'a good girl'. I'd once seen her secreting a twenty-pound note, handed to her by a spotty youth, and I suspect it was a payment for drugs. She claimed to have a British husband, father of her three-year-old. He never seemed to be around. Perhaps he was in prison. I didn't like to ask.

By the time Fumi and I got back after washing up, the police had been called and the interrogation was about to begin. Our 'woman police officer', presumably appointed by Barbara Edwards, was Claudia, a Polish lady, who'd been coming to the class for as long as I'd been leading the group. She wisely ignored Natasha, who was a prime suspect because she'd been helping Fumi prepare the coffee, and instead she directed her questions to timid Fumi, who spoke perfect English.

"Do you always make the coffee for the class?"

"No, er, yes, er, no, er, sometimes."

'Sometimes' was the safe answer. Fumi read Dickens and Shakespeare but was a hesitant speaker. I wondered whether she always understood what was said to her.

With trepidation, I watched police attention focus upon Natasha, who reacted aggressively: "Why you say, 'vot your name'?" she demanded.

I felt my temper rising and sat with my hands supporting my face so that no one could see my expression.

"I donnow 'your name'." Her broad shoulders in the expensive sweater shrugged, "Is 'Sergeant Po Lease'?"

"What is your name?" repeated our patient police lady.

"Vot you vant? My name? Your name?"

She'd done this before: pretending she didn't understand the simplest things. It was just a game or maybe it was how she dealt with the police in real life. She must have a smattering of at least three other languages. Or had she never conversed with those previous husbands of hers, each from a different continent? The skin tones of her beautiful children, evenly colour-coded according to age, attested to her various liaisons. The eldest, brightest and blackest, was doing medical research at London University.

Policewoman Claudia cut the time-wasting.

"Write your name, address and telephone number on this piece of paper."

Natasha's gravelly voice drowned out other conversation.

"A piece of ...vot? Ah yes, piece off! My school daughter always say me 'Piss off, Mum!'" Her chuckle was as warm and wicked as treacle.

Our policewoman continued almost faultlessly: "The murder victim, Mrs Edwards, does not usually attend this class. You do not know her before today. Who has the motive for to murder of her? And, by the way, who removed the coffee cup and washed it up?"

"Teacher!" shouted Natasha.

"The two ladies in the kitchen, Fumi and Natasha, had the opportunity to put poison into the cup? You say the lights went out for a short time."

Olga, wife of a famous Russian dissident, explained that Jenny had gone to turn on more lights because it came over very dark,

"..but she, Jenny, confuses and she switches and she turns all them off by mistake. It is not very dark but we cannot see very well for a few moments."

I smiled, nodded and mouthed 'very good' to Olga. Third person singular present tense was the grammar we'd been practising earlier.

"I in kitchen, I seed Teacher do like this." Natasha is determined to implicate me in the crime.

Policewoman Claudia turned to the two Chinese ladies. "Please explain me what you see."

They giggled and looked at each other. Then the elder said,

"Natasha quite light. When rights go out: Teacher, she moves all the cups. She gives poison to Mrs School Inspector Barbara."

"Not Jenny," stated the younger Chinese, shaking her head vigorously. "Everybody move the cups but not Jenny."

"So, perhaps the School Inspector, Mrs Edwards, drinks the poison by mistake. Perhaps she is not the intended victim! Now I'm going to ask each person to say who they think is the intended victim, what is the motive for the crime."

"Every people have motive." Natasha pointed. "She and she and she. I tell you...."

This time, the whole class hissed her into silence.

I was really delighted with the way the role play was going. Just last week we'd played my version of Cluedo and I'd asked Claudia to play the role of the police inspector; she must have kept the list of phrases and vocabulary that I'd handed out. Barbara Edwards must surely be impressed.

At that point, I noticed Barbara Edwards was still slumped against the sofa playing the part of the victim and 'acting dead' instead of taking notes on all the grammar mistakes as I would have expected.

In class, I encourage the students to use their imaginations when answering questions. There is no obligation for them to reveal their personal details about their real lives. Many could relate very traumatic events that had happened to them before arriving in this country. "You do not have to tell us the truth about yourself or your family," I say. "Only if you want to." - Most do tell the truth because it's easier than inventing a lie. - "For example," I tell them, "when I ask you if you own a pet you can pretend to have a lion cub or a race horse - anything you like to imagine."

However, at the end of a question and answer session, I usually ask them to confess if they've lied. Usually they say it's all true. Sometimes their confessions are hardly believable, but again, it's up to them. So long as they say something, that's all that matters. Communication is what it's all about.

"I suspect that the poisoned coffee was intended for Natasha...." began Olga.

"Me, why me? No body want bloodyell kill me!"

Olga continued, "...because she disrupts the class and because she is involved in a drug-running syndicate...."

"Is lies! Is all lies! You say me bad things, I take you to court! Is Olga. She THE murdering! BE Kosofo, in THE war Mrs Polinski husband is murdering to Olga husband. Is right, is right, I tell you!"

I gave Natasha a look that would have turned anyone else to stone.

"Sorry, Teacher."

Natasha's whisper drowned the beginning of Fumi's suggestion that there is a deadly rivalry between the Chinese and Bangladeshi restaurant owners. Wife-poisoning, it seems, had become more fashionable than kidnapping as a way of frightening off the competition.

"Women do not kill people on behalf of their husbands," stated our Vietnamese graduate student. "Motives for women are always sexual."

I glanced towards Natasha, expecting an interruption. Her attention was riveted, for some reason, upon Jenny.

The Vietnamese continued: "One of the ladies here wishes to remove permanently another lady because she wants to marry this lady's husband. The question you should be asking, madam police officer, is this: which of us has a husband sufficiently attractive, either physically or in terms of money or property, to make a woman wish to commit murder to get him?"

"Neither physical beauty nor money," Mrs Shah's voice was so soft and sweet, "is necessary for love and marriage."

" Quite right, Mrs Shah," encouraged Jenny, whose husband, incidentally, was both good-looking and wealthy.

Natasha could not contain herself any longer,

"O.K. anybody wan' my husband? She can have him! Free offer. I no mind. I like a different husband now, I think… Very younger, more good at THE sex. Yes. Very much strong and young. So is no me she try to kill."

"Some woman is very jealous," began Mrs Polinski, "and she murder the other woman. For this type of a killing is no death penalty in England. A woman, jealous, unhappy, she say herself,

'Murdering this girl, who steal my husband, is good idea.'"

"Jealousy is the motive," affirmed Olga.

"Hey look, you know vot? I sink is the po lease. She, done the murdering." Natasha pointed an accusing crimson nail at Claudia. "In my country is always the po lease. You know why? They only men with guns."

"But the police in England do not have guns."

"No guns, so poison. Po leaseman Claudia, she poison with coffee! Aha! Yes! We, all class say po leaseman Claudia do THE murdering. Everybody all say, 'Yeeees!'"

Obediently most of the students said: "Yeees!"

"Good! All finished, Teacher. Jolly good show! Claudia spitting image of po leaseman. Everybody all clap for Claudia! Hands clap!"

Amazingly they did.

"Why you make we to do this murdering-play, Teacher? Eh? We all stinking afryed of po lease. Look Mrs Polinski hand, her hand nervous, shy king. Mrs Polinski shy of King, and very shy of po lease. And in Chile, po lease murdering to Maria all her family! Eh? So every body in this class have bad time in her country with po lease. No Fumi. Fumi have bad time with Mr Fumi." That wicked chuckle again. "Why you make us to do this murdering-play, Teacher?"

I protested that everyone had agreed that playing Cluedo was a good idea when it was suggested last week.

"I tell you why is no good idea. Is no role-play for poor Mrs Barbara, lying there, very quiet. No sleeping. No writing bad things on THE class. THE school inspector she look dead, good and proper!"

She lifted Barbara's arm and let it fall.

There was panic, screaming and fainting. My hands were 'shy king' and I was 'stinking afryed' myself.

The ambulance arrived in five minutes and we were given to understand that there was every chance Barbara Edwards would make a full recovery.

Someone had also called the police.

Until the official interpreters arrived, I had to help the police with the questioning of my terror-stricken students. Some of them began repeating the highly improbable stories they'd concocted about one another for their role-play, which we'd devised to impress the visiting school inspector, and now, poor Barbara Edwards, our volunteer victim, was perhaps really and truly, nearly dead.

What with the language problems and the imaginary motives, and the distrust and fear, the police were utterly confused. At last they said we could all go home.

After I'd tidied up, I was in a state of collapse. I'd just made myself a cup of tea when Natasha reappeared and sat next to me.

"The po lease, they is thinking you is THE murdering. Donna worry, Teacher. No is poisoning with this coffee. Is strong drug in little cut, like injection for animals. I seed CIA/ KGB use this injection in my country. Mrs Barbara carn move, like piss off wood, carn talk. Is drug. Donna worry, Teacher, if po lease take you for prison, I tell them: 'No!' - I see everything very quickly. I know who is real true murdering."

I smiled and thanked her.

"THE motive is jealousy. THE lady is murdering her husband BE Kosofo he is no-good-play-around boy. I see in THE face how she bloodyell ATE Mrs Barabara, terrible bloodyell ATE Mrs Barbara. I guess Mrs Barbara she try to steal from THE lady her no-good husband."

She sighed.

"My number three husband, he no damn good. I murdering him, you know. I murdering him because he bloodyell terrible man."

She brightened up.

"I no tell po lease which is THE lady murdering, O.K.? If po lease muck up things, and they say you murdering Mrs Barbara, then I tell THE truth."

She put her arm round me and almost murdered me in her crushing hug.

The trouble was, now I too guessed the identity of the murderess. Jenny's handsome, veterinary surgeon husband kept drugs for immobilizing animals. He had been treating Barbara Edwards's dogs. I'd seen his car outside her house at all hours.

Had Jenny hoped to confuse the police with all the lies that we'd encouraged our students to think up about each other; all those fictitious crimes, grudges and supposed blackmails that we'd practised together last week?

We were all poisoned now. The class could never survive this terrible ordeal.

"Cheer up," said Natasha, with a wink. "Donna worry, Teacher, I tell them: 'You come'. They all come to class on next week. You see."

And so they did.

And so did Jenny.

The school inspector, Mrs Barbara Edwards, eventually recovered. Apparently, she told the police

she thought she had not been the intended victim.
But who knows?

# 11  Basil of the Buses

A good actor would have problems mimicking the lacklustre delivery of the words welcoming Intercity Coach travellers. Alas, that our own dear Peter Sellers is no longer with us to exactly capture the driver's dull, yet exasperated tones, redolent with the suppressed misery of being obliged, under Company Rule xxx, to mouth these words:-

"Star-Bus Company welcomes you aboard the nine-forty-five Star-bus from Heathrow...." Sir Mel or Sir Warren or Sir Kenneth might continue:- "...which is running EIGHTEEN minutes LATE....."

No, no. Sorry to have to stop you there, Sir Mel. You have to realise that this is the part of his job he really enjoys. It's the only glimmer that approaches happiness in his tawdry existence. It's what gets him up in the morning and almost brings a smirk to his face as he slams his front door and kicks at the blue crisp packet - that single touch of colour in the drab debris of torn cellophane, dirty tissues and sodden flyers that litters his winter-derelict front garden....

He has his passengers, his Returning Passengers, docile from the slaughter-house regime of the air-lines, meek with jet-lag, sorrowful to the point of tears with lost love, and terminally depressed at the prospect of returning to work, possibly later that very same day despite the jet-lag, the queasy tummy, the desperate broken-heartache - and the headache - and no spare money left at the end of it all.

Ho ho, our Basil Fawlty has bad news to deliver to his Returning Passengers. He has them, broken and at his mercy - or so he thinks.

Mel darling, sorry, you've haven't quite got enough covert glee resonating in the long, flat vowel of that word 'late'.

The driver speaks slowly and deliberately because there might be sub-human foreigners with a poor grasp of English on board.

"I must warn passenger that we shall be LATE arriving at our destination. This is due, of course, to TRAFFIC conditions, (a sigh to indicate that this is normal) and to having to (sniffs bitterly) WRITE TICKETS."

Here there is a pregnant pause so that offending ticket buyers might, despite weariness etc, cotton onto the fact that he dislikes writing tickets and that everyone else on board is forced to suffer a degree of lateness because of their criminal negligence in not managing to acquire a ticket before boarding the bus.

"At present we are running NINETEEN minutes LATE but we could be considerably LATER depending on the fog, the traffic conditions and, of course, (sigh) on the number of TICKETS that have to be WRITTEN."

Passengers in the know wink and nudge one another. They smile and settle back to enjoy the entertainment. Good old England. During their lapse abroad, they'd forgotten all about the British sense of humour, about Basil Fawlty and his Charm School in which so many of the welcoming committee of British salt-of-the-earth functionaries have learned their public relations skills. For example:-

"Oy! What d'you think you're doing? Oy! You can't stand there!" etc.

The last passenger in the queue, now shamefully clutching his just-acquired ticket, tries not to accidentally knock into anyone with his hand-luggage or catch the strap on an armrest as he side-shuffles along the narrow aisle looking for a spare seat.

Outside the bus, a passenger has just emerged from the lift/elevator. His mind is still on the other side of the world as he pushes the recalcitrant trolley/wagonette loaded with toppling bags. Suddenly he looks up and notices the place name on the front of the coach. He had not expected to catch this coach. He was resigned to an hour's wait but slowly the significance of the bus with the destination writ large above the driver's window penetrates his consciousness and evinces a sudden suicidal desire to avail himself of this stroke of luck.

The coach driver has noticed all this. He closes the doors and switches on the engine but the coach does not move yet. Perhaps he is waiting for his last passenger to settle into his seat before releasing the brake.

Bus drivers all over the world wish to teach late passengers a lesson - so to encourage this late-comer in his fantasy, our driver waits a little longer. The trolley comes hurtling along the pavement/sidewalk. The belt of his white American/German raincoat is about to fall out of its tab, the duty-frees clink dangerously. Of course he'll have no ticket. It will have to be WRITTEN. We old-hands all know he hasn't a hope in hell. The coach engine throbs into life, then dies away as though it's going to stop and wait for him. The trolley-pusher smiles in precocious gratitude and rushes recklessly on, demonstrating his consideration for others and the desire not to hold up the coach. But the easing off of the throttle was only to change gear. At exactly the right moment, the coach heaves itself into motion and pulls away from Terminal Four bus station twenty minutes late.

The coach moves rapidly, tyres hissing on the damp, grey road beyond the canopy. Behind us we watch the trolley, its burden already shifted by the unsuitable haste into imminent instability, catastrophically descend the ramp into the road where it jettisons matching baggage in the path of a hotel courtesy minibus.

Rest assured, it takes more than this minor triumph to pierce the armour of our driver's misanthropy. After issuing the welcome quoted above, he continues: "I am required to inform you that all passengers must remain seated at all times. No smoking WHATSOEVER is allowed on this coach. The regulations require that all hand-baggage MUST be stored in the overhead compartments or under the seats." He pauses. The sound of his deep sigh comes over the intercom. Very slowly and clearly, for the sake of imbecilic foreigners who haven't the intelligence to learn English like a native, he repeats his last remark about hand-luggage. Then, gritting his teeth around his smouldering anger: "Will the person at the back of the coach kindly conform with the regulations and remove his bag from the centre aisle immediately."

There's a pause in the in-coach entertainment during which a stifled titter can be heard at the back of the class. Like a mischievous child, a humorous passenger has been testing the limits, perhaps?

"Thank you, Sir." Flames of rage spurt from Basil's nostril and singe the microphone.

The coach continues in silence for a while. Visibility is not bad enough to slow the mesh of London-circulating traffic. To the front and rear and each side of the coach are cars, lorries, motorbikes and other coaches, all filthy from the film of mud being thrown up by the tyres, all progressing at speed with minimal space between them. The grass is bright green. Everything else is various shades of grey. The heat on the coach is intolerable.

A girl in the second row behind the driver leans forward and asks the girl in front of her to request the driver to turn down the heating or adjust the ventilation. The whole coach waits: a truly dramatic moment. Will she have the guts? Yes. Naive as Dickens' Oliver Twist, there she is, leaning over, talking to the driver. This is a courageous act. It contravenes the regulations clearly printed and displayed above the driver's head stating that the driver must not be spoken to or otherwise distracted. Will he order a flogging? We cannot hear what she is saying. We cannot hear what the driver replies.

The intercom system splutters into life: "Everything that can be switched on in this coach is switched on."

Quite a mild response! The girl who mentioned the heating to the driver must be a diplomat returning from Brussels. The hot girl removes her sweater and sits in her camisole top. Other people have already removed various garments. The coach with its occupants has taken on the appearance of lunch-time in a London park during a heat wave. Heat-induced lethargy lulls the passengers into a state of compliance. Some may actually have passed out but there are not many of us on the coach so the oxygen is not yet depleted. Any body odour that may be evaporating into the desert-dry air is masked by the smell of hot rubber and burning dust.

Suddenly there is a sound like machine-gun fire and we start up from our slumped positions, eyes wild with terror. In our absence, has England too become subject to guerrilla attacks? No need to worry, it's only a radio communication with another coach driver enquiring about the fog and traffic conditions.

"What time are you getting in?" the other driver asks ours.

"Soon as possible."

Crackle, splifsths.... "This morning? Need you ask?" Splutter, phut....

"Five Hours. I've had enough of this lark." Crunckle.....

"I'm jacking in this effing job." Zup, tattetle-tat....

"Too right...."

We are approaching the Central Bus Station at Heathrow Terminals One, Two and Three. The old hands on board try to rouse themselves to be ready for any entertainment that might be on offer with the arrival of more Returning Passengers. We are not disappointed.

"Here we go. Right then." Our driver flops out of the bus to supervise the loading of the luggage into the compartments underneath.

"Okay! Now which of you…?'

No, no, Mel, (our world-famous actor would have further problems with the nuances of intonation in his attempt to portray this fascinating character.) What we need here, Mel, is even more exasperation in the tone, right?

"Which one of you got onto the bus while I was round the back loading the baggage?"

Our driver struggles to keep the eagerness out of his voice. This has really made it all worthwhile. Despite the fume-filled, grinding trail through the fog, the hold-ups in dense traffic, the meagre monetary reward, there are compensations. This is where job-satisfaction really comes into its own. Dealing with badly-behaved passengers, that's the high spot.

'Don't own up,' we, the innocent, urge under our breath. Will it be like school? Shall we have to wait here at Heathrow's main terminal until someone volunteers to take the rap?

A girl in a thin, summery cardigan stands up. She is pale, ill-looking, in other words, a typical Returning Passenger.

His eyes almost betray his joy at finding the culprit is a woman. "Do you realise your action could get me dismissed?"

How was it that a crescendo of applause, cheers, whistles and laughter never happened?

"Entering the bus in the driver's absence," he lectures, "is an infringement of the regulations. Attempting to travel WITHOUT a TICKET is a serious offence."

The girl is apologizing and opening her purse. Obviously a ticket will have to be WRITTEN. We gasp delightedly at the horror of it.

"I'm sorry." She speaks loudly so that the rest of us can hear. "I didn't know. It was cold so I got inside. My coat's just been stolen and I..."

"Ah ha, don't give me that. Telling sob stories now, are we? I know all the tricks, all your pathetic ways of trying it on... You don't fool me, my dear..."

And then he turns her off the bus and makes her wait outside in the cold fog behind all the other passengers who have formed a queue to get onto the coach. Some have tickets but for various other miscreants who have arrived in England without them, he has to WRITE out more TICKETS.

Finally the girl in the pale pink cotton top is sitting down. We sink back in our seats surprised and even perhaps, like a blood-sport crowd cheated of its amusement (guillotine malfunction), a little disappointed that he has not reprimanded her afresh. However, the entertainment provided by the bus company to welcome visitors to England and give them a taste of the joys in store, is not over yet, oh no, not by a long chalk.

The coach is not drawing away from the coach station. Instead, the driver chooses to indulge in making a series of announcements. If we were more observant we might realise why he's doing this.

"Due to traffic congestion and the writing of TICKETS, our expected arrival time has been further DELAYED. We shall now be thirty minutes LATE arriving at our destination. It is my duty to inform you that some police authorities routinely prosecute people seated in the last four and the first three rows on coaches who are NOT wearing seat belts. It is entirely up to individual passengers whether they wish to obey the LAW or not. I cannot be held responsible. I merely inform passengers of this likelihood."

The coach door has been left open as an enticing trap for a young man who climbs onto the first step. He's carrying a large backpack.

"Could you open the back so that I can put this in, please?"

"No."

"Oh. It's all right for me to bring this inside, then?"

"All hand luggage must be stowed under the seats or in the overhead lockers."

The polite young man puts his foot on the second step.

"Will that go under the seats?"

Befuddled, the young man gazes along the rows of seats, hoping to see one that's high enough off the ground to accommodate his possessions.

"You can't bring that inside," states the driver.

"Oh, well, then..."

His foot retreats from the second step and he is on the point of repeating his request for an opening of the luggage compartment. He's a Returner. He's exhausted but he's experienced many encounters with power-crazy minor bureaucrats at distant customs posts.

"You don't want me to travel on this coach?"

"That depends on whether you want to leave your luggage behind. There'll be another bus along in half-an hour, that is, if it's not ALSO running LATE."

"Right. Fair enough." The habit of not getting on the wrong side of petty officials takes a while to wear off. One forgets that British jails are too full to land up there, simply for shouting and making a fuss.

Fuss is embarrassing. The English, in the past, would rarely make a scene. Too easily they see the other fella's point of view. The bus is running late. It will take at least a minute for the driver to get out and unlock the back and supervise the loading - or probably it's a rule that the driver must personally stow the baggage. A whole minute, maybe several minutes, will be lost. A driver is not obliged to take passengers – for example, ones who are drunk.

However, not all the spunk has deserted our Returners. Not all English people are quietly compromising by taking off their sweaters and shirts to sit in their vests throughout the journey.

"Oh, come o-on," a voice from the middle of the bus wheedles in the style of: 'Go on be a sport, Sir. Pleeease Sir."

The door-closing mechanism hisses at the young man who says, "Fine, o.k." as he steps back into the wintery morning.

An ominous murmuring and shuffling is taking place amongst the company.

"Oh, let him on, for goodness sake," a bored voice plans to make it nothing too important.

"There's plenty of room. If you let him on with his pack, we won't report you," says a young woman. Possibly this remark contains a veiled threat?

The engine churns into life. Voices of protest are raised on all sides.

The driver's flat, official voice blares over the intercom in an attempt to drown out the angry outbursts that come from all over the bus. People in vests and without them are getting up. Passengers are out of their seats, standing in the aisle with their trousers and sleeves rolled up. A middle-aged Scottish woman, waving her tights and slip, is screeching out the fury and outrage they all feel. It's mob rule. The passengers are refusing to resume their seats until the young man with the backpack is allowed on board.

Our driver is not disconcerted. He switches off the engine.

"If that's the way you want it, it's all right by me. We can sit here all day, if you like, though I'm sure you have friends and family, if not business commitments, awaiting your arrival. I'm within my rights. I'll just call up the headquarters of the bus company and inform them of the situation. I trust this will not become a police matter."

But he's too late. The girl behind him has leaned over and grabbed his microphone. It's ripped out and passed to the back of the bus.

"Now that's a very serious offence," warns the driver. "I have no alternative but to request that you leave this vehicle immediately, young woman - and that goes for anyone else who's thinking of causing trouble."

He still hasn't realised the degree of hostility towards him.

"Disruptive elements may be ejected at my discretion. I am not obliged to carry anyone. Now either you sit down and behave or you get off my bus." He waits. "I'm warning you....."

His orders are drowned by jeers which include: 'Little Hitler', 'over-ripe turd' and 'bumptious little pip-squeak'. Courageously he faces the horde, who are now mindless with rage.

"Let's grab him," a delicate student-type with loosened tie urges a couple of tattooed lads.

"Pleasure, Man," they grin and the bus driver is up-ended over the back of his seat.

"I don't mind driving," offers an ancient librarian.

"No Dad, that's o.k. I got a licence. Shall we stuff him in the boot?

"Well, I don't think..."

"Yes," scream the others, cheering and clapping.

The hydraulic coach door opens and Basil of the buses is lifted off his feet by well-muscled youths and he's carried, protesting and struggling, outside. Other passengers drag the young man with the large backpack inside. Rather mystified, he receives a hero's welcome. The driver screams vengeance, as he's bundled into the luggage compartment. The journey is resumed. The heating is turned down.

When we arrive at our destination, we group around the opened luggage compartment to collect our luggage and to release driver. But before the young wrestlers give him back his shoes and his braces he has to wait and listen while we all make a solemn vow to never breathe a word about this mutiny to a living soul. We each swear that, if need be, we shall commit perjury, and we'll lie our heads off even under torture. Even the group-minded Japanese nod vehemently in agreement and take the oath. Our solidarity is unanimous; it's 'all for one and one for all.'

So, as far as anyone else knows, nothing untoward actually occurred during that journey from Heathrow.

Never believe your friends when they claim their trip to anywhere was uneventful. There must be something they're not telling you.

# 12 Emoji for a World Wrung Dry

Long ago, my husband and I were travelling in a far-off land where the ancient customs were valued, at least by our high-ranking host. I doubt the servants, resplendent in their waiting-at-table scarlet and gold, were entirely enthusiastic – but you never know - they did, after all, have employment and they got to dress up occasionally as though they were extras in some old Hollywood drama.

We humble academics were seated as honoured guests on this lavishly appointed table only because we were on holiday with our old college friend, Angus - not his real name - who had known our wealthy host since public school. Over the intervening years they'd kept in touch: Angus would invite Duckee to shoot grouse over his grandfather's purple heather and Duckee would invite Angus to come and kill far more exotic game in his faraway eastern neck of the woods.

Not being remotely moneyed, Jeff and I felt rather out of our depth but this was a grand opportunity to experience what it felt like to be waited on by white-gloved minions and eat off precious porcelain dishes whilst portraits of ancestors peered down their noses at us from the panelled walls. I intended to savour every aspect of the evening.

I'd borrowed a long gown in a suitably dismal shade and I'd under-gone a session at the hairdressers that left me with hair stiffened to twice its normal size. Those were the days before scientists had decided that the chemicals in aerosols were depleting the ozone layer, causing an increased risk of skin cancer.

Once our handsome host had ascertained that I wasn't wittily flirtatious or sexually alluring - despite the amount of cleavage revealed by the borrowed plunging neck-line, he turned to my husband and began quizzing him about a catastrophic decline in the population of his most treasured game species: 'Might there be a fertility problem among the males?' he asked, followed by more queries such as: 'Should fertiliser be sprayed over the pasture?' and 'How bad is the poaching in Africa?'

Aha, the penny dropped: Angus had wangled us an invitation to the ancestral abode of his foreign friend because Duckee desperately needed advice from my conservation-environmentalist husband.

Jeff is always scientifically cautious when giving his opinions – none of your tabloid-press sensational easy solutions; he'd never advocate the death penalty for illegal loggers or poachers. I guess Angus would have warned Jeff to research the local issues and he'd have known the annual rainfall and temperature fluctuations over the past decade, but

Jeff's tactic was to appear ill-informed and to question his host in such a way as to encourage him think like a conservationist rather than a hunter.

Jeff was in his element. I'd heard it all many times before so I turned to Angus, but he was intent on following my husband's technique. 'Jeff's the right man for this delicate job,' he whispered to me.

Jeff began by admiring the gruesome animal trophies decorating the walls: 'How long ago was the finest trophy shot? Where...? How...?'

Duckee was only too happy to recount the hunting exploits of his father and grandfather. In those days game had been abundant. He was a charming raconteur and breathtakingly good-looking with it. The whole table fell silent to listen to his hair-raising accounts of near-disastrous hunting expeditions.

'And what about these days?' Jeff enquired. 'The size of the antlers, for example...'

The wealthy hunter pursed his lips and shook his head. 'Bad, very poor....' and he explained how difficult it was to find suitably large animals for his privileged guests to shoot.

I concentrated on the many interesting dishes that were placed before us. Each course was accompanied by a different wine. Then I overheard Jeff mention a stuffed giant pangolin in the entrance lobby. He had to describe the scaley ant-eater before Duckee could recall that his father had brought it back from a hunting expedition to East Africa.

'Pangolin scales are greatly prized among the Chinese community for their medicinal and aphrodisiac properties,' said Duckee, glancing at my cleavage before fixing me with his beautiful dark eyes to watch my reaction. By this time, much wine had been consumed; the white gloves were removing the fourth or possibly fifth course. Duckee looked slightly annoyed when he noticed that I'd only sipped a little from each of the glasses clustered around my plate. He indicated that the waiter should remove them.

'A pangolin's claws are powerful enough to rip open hard-baked termite mounds on the African savannah…' Jeff was spouting his stuff. 'The spectacular giant pangolin must perform a vital function in the complex interplay of life in a grassland habitat. Of course, to understand all the implications, further research is needed.'

At this point, Lucy, one of Duckee's cousins who'd been introduced to us as a biology graduate from Stanford, suggested that: 'Breaking open the termite mounds would enable birds and other animals to access a rich feast of termite grubs.'

'Exactly,' said my husband leaning forward to bestow a beaming smile of encouragement upon his new-found ally. 'Who knows how vital that food source might be for the survival of those species. As you know, the smaller tree pangolin is being mercilessly persecuted by poachers to meet an ever-increasing demand for its scales.'

He did not mention that the dusty item of taxidermy lurking in a dark corner of the hallway was probably worth to animal traffickers the equivalent of what Duckee had paid for his latest sports car. Sadly, a few months later we heard that the stuffed pangolin had disappeared. Duckee immediately warned various natural history and zoological museums not to display their pangolins. Now there are only wax models to be seen next to cards regretting that the original is locked in a bank vault.

'If these small defenceless mammals were to disappear from the forests, the ants on which they feed might possibly become a serious pest. Unchecked by predation, termites could wreak havoc upon trees... the forests could become sparse and eventually disappear... who knows? And without the protection of the forest canopy, the heavy seasonal rains will wash away the soil creating an environmental catastrophe leading eventually to famine and desert conditions.'

There was a gasp and whispering among the other guests, some of whom belonged to the Chinese community.

'Ants can be controlled with pesticides,' remarked someone at the end of the table.

Jeff ignored this and continued: 'We have to assume that all creatures, however insignificant they may appear, contribute in wonderful, sometimes mysterious, ways to the overall health of the ecosystem. Incidentally, termites, as well as other creatures that live on the forest floor, are superb at removing plant debris, thus helping to reduce the risk of forest fires. I'll give you a few more examples of the unexpected benefits...'

These days his animal stories may be familiar to viewers of nature programmes on television but back then they were all new.

For example, he described how termites cultivate a fungus to break down the cellulose in wood. 'Nutrients are in short supply and must be recycled as quickly as possible...'

I watched Jeff rapidly swallowing the various courses during dramatic pauses in his narrative and swilling them down with the accompanying wines. I hoped that his alcohol intake wasn't impairing his sensitivity to the effect his words were having on our host and his influential guests. Usually my husband remains cool and, in my opinion, he's far too moderate and judicial when expressing his thoughts on any controversial issue but on that particular evening he grew evermore passionate as he explained that the loss of any species is detrimental to the whole: 'For our own survival, ecosystems must continue to work at their most efficient and for that it's important that every aspect of the habitat, even the most trivial, is preserved ...'

Was Jeff miscalculating his audience's reaction? He must have known that much of Duckee's family wealth was derived from the timber plundered from ancient tropical rainforests?

'Nature recycles everything: the water we depend on for our crops, the oxygen we breathe, the carbon we burn for energy, nitrogen, phosphorous, everything is reused, time after time, and yet, apparently, we human beings have never noticed this. Like children we think all resources are limitless; that our parents, or the gods, will always provide whatever we need; our food, our fuel will always miraculously be there. We should learn from nature and note how cleverly the world functions: how it has always recycled. Instead of which: we take, we use, we throw away.'

I sensed a change in the atmosphere. Had Jeff not noticed how the handsome young face of our host had hardened with displeasure?

'We've exploited the natural world ever since we began to hunt. Remember all those animals gone forever, never to be recovered: the dodo, the mammoth, the passenger pigeon...'

- Remember: all this took place way back in the early seventies, long before the effects of climate change became obvious to everyone -

'...We are no longer children. We understand that there is a limit to resources. You, Duckee, and some of your friends here, are in a unique position to repair the damage that the forests may have suffered. Nature can repair itself to a great extent, if given half a chance, if the cancer is caught in time. Your beautiful animals need their pristine forests to recover their vitality and survive.'

I watched Duckee's hand turn into a fist gripping his napkin. He was really angry. If only I could think of some jokey remark to distract him!

'If it were not for my grandfather, no wildlife would remain...' Duckee muttered, belligerently defensive. I could feel the heat coming off him.

'People of your calibre could possibly save the planet from total collapse if you were prepared to, for example, limit the use of pesticides, consider what happens to non-degradable fabrics, reduce the use of fossil fuels that pollute the air and cause acid rain...'

I glanced at the man beside me – he was bright scarlet, chewing his cheeks, swallowing hard, snorting deep breaths, fists clenched before him on the table. This was not the answer he wanted. He'd like to increase the use of chemicals to solve problems not reduce them. Any minute he'd explode or worse. Did they still fight duels in this country, I wondered, or would he order assassins to dispose of his ungracious guest?

Then, as though to prevent some unseemly confrontation, the most ornate of the attendants bent forward and whispered something to our host.

Duckee leaped to his feet and forced himself to smile. His fists thudded the table for silence. People had been discussing Jeff's remarks. Poor Angus, I thought, I hope we've not queered his pitch, but when I turned around, Angus was nodding in approval and gesturing a silent applause.

Our host cleared his throat and with supreme effort controlled his temper. 'Ah yes, dear friends,' he began rather hoarsely. 'Now the time has come for the presentation of our final and extremely special dish. And so, ladies and gentlemen, let us introduce a change of mood, perhaps, a change of topic.' He glared at Jeff, who was still beaming, a little drunk perhaps and certainly euphoric with passionate enthusiasm for the subject that was closest to his heart. He seemed completely unaware that he'd caused great offence.

'This truly delicious dessert, which we call the nurse's pudding, consists of tropical wild fruits gathered from our forest trees. These are eaten with, or should I say they are accompanied by, as you will see, small round pastries. To add a certain delicate sweetness, these pastries have been steeped in human breastmilk expressed from the voluptuous breasts of most generous nursing mothers. This prestigious dish was formerly served only to emperors or princes – and on one occasion, I believe, to a member of your own dear royal family who honoured us with his presence during an arduous hunting expedition. This noblest of desserts confers longevity and good health. Bon appetit!

I felt we should maybe have clapped a welcome when some really unusual plates appeared before us –a ceramic curve divided the berries from the tiny pastries. Of course, I convinced myself that the soggy pastry had not really been contaminated with human breastmilk.

As Duckee sat down he leaned over me and whispered: 'It is especially nutritious for women of a certain age. They say it vastly improves their libido.'

Blushing hot with fury, I was about to retaliate but I didn't get the chance because Duckee suddenly went berserk.

He was standing up again, yelling and screaming and pounding the table. He had turned from a smooth, delightful young man into a hideous monster. Something about the dish was obviously not to his liking. What was wrong and what he was demanding we had no idea. The servants rushed around gathering up the untouched plates and lining them up on the sideboard. We watched in confusion as Duckee paced up and down gesticulating as he waited for something or someone to appear.

'Hi Duckee, what's wrong,' Angus called several times. At last a morose reply was given: 'Too cold. The idiots did not get them out of the fridge ahead of time.' Duckee returned to the table. 'Sorry for the delay, my friends. I should explain: the pastries must be served at blood temperature; it is imperative.'

There was a shuffling movement among the huddle of attendants by the door. Then the scarlet and gold uniforms parted to reveal a small woman dressed in the local peasant costume: a brightly patterned skirt and crisp white blouse with puffed sleeves and a drawstring top. Had she been waiting on standby?

'Ah, splendid, come here, my dear.' Our host beckoned her to approach as he stood beside the first of the dessert plates lined up along the sideboard. She walked towards him untying the top of her blouse, loosening it so that she could bring out her enormous breast engorged with milk.

Duckee said something to the woman who leaned forward slightly and allowed him to cup her breast in his right hand. He then began to squeeze as though he held a grapefruit or a smooth, weighty beef-steak tomato. The bluish milk squirted out amazingly all over the dessert plates that were shuffled forward by the white-gloved waiters and distributed among the guests, once Duckee deemed the little pastries were sufficiently warmed up. The second breast was soaking milk through the cloth of the blouse. The woman insisted on its being used. My god, she must have been in agony. My own breasts were throbbing in painful sympathy. I can never erase from my mind the horrifying image of a male hand grasping that great glistening globe and squeezing the life-giving milk out of it.

I felt someone gripping my elbow, trying to attract my attention. It was Duckee's great aunt, the hostess. She quietly indicated that the ladies should retire and leave the gentlemen to their cigars and 'naughty jokes'.

Later, as we took tea on the other side of the building, Lucy the biology graduate said:

'Well, my upon word, Ladies, and doesn't that hand gripping the breast just sum up exactly what these men are doing to our planet? They don't seem to realise our children will suffer. All that concerns them is making a profit today; they disregard the disastrous consequences of their actions.'

We considered this analogy.

Lucy continued: 'The rules in the Game of Life can always be changed. Let us hope that a new order will soon be established where concern for the welfare of the planet is more prestigious than …'

'But alas,' interrupted her grandmother, 'only the rich are powerful enough to alter the system. In the United States, where everyone is supposed to have been created equal, they changed the rules so the equality rule did not apply to slaves.'

'The Nazis also changed the rules to exclude the Jews but they had seized power because the rich had failed to control the financial situation,' Lucy stated. 'When my brother kept changing the rules in his Pokémon game, I refused to play with him. We should refuse to play the Game of Life with these destroyers of our planet.'

'If you were a totalitarian regime you could enforce changes to the rules,' said her grandmother. 'In democracies, it is more difficult…'

'Only because some countries are run entirely for the benefit of the wealthy…' interrupted Lucy.

'Which is why Jeff and I came here this evening…' I said. 'Maybe if your husbands really understood the situation, they would change the rules to benefit the long-term health of our planet.'

All this happened a very long time ago but very little has changed in the last fifty years: very few environmental regulations have been implemented. People tend to lack the ideas and the initiative to enact new systems. The aspiration of our grandparents, many of which caused our present predicament, are still revered but we must reconsider our traditional ways of evaluating people's worth. Change must come if disaster is to be averted.

# 13  A Dream Comes True

What are those two young children doing on this cross-channel ferry all on their own, you may be asking, as you watch the stewardess go into their little cabin in the middle of the night.

Even in summer, the North Sea can be a bit rough and the poor little younger one, Polly, was feeling very seasick so she'd rung the bell to call the stewardess who was looking after them. Her sister, Penny, who was two years older, refused to admit that she also felt a bit queasy. This was because going on a sea voyage was what she had always wanted to do: it was a dream come true.

When the letter first arrived, it seemed as though they would never be allowed to accept the kind invitation. Willy, pronounced Villy, had written inviting the schoolgirls to stay with her family in Holland for four whole weeks in the summer. Willy, who spoke excellent English, had stayed with them in England while she was thinking about working here – or while she was recovering from a broken love-affair, as the mother of Penny and Polly suspected.

Twelve-year-old Penny was told that she couldn't go to Holland on her own. 'And,' added her mother, 'Polly is much too young to be away from home.' She naturally couldn't bear to be apart from her children. 'You know how Polly can be a bit of a handful.'

'But during the war, children younger than Polly were evacuated, weren't they? And Trudy was only a year older than I am now when she came to stay with us on her own for two months.'

'And you remember how homesick she was and how she cried for her Mummy that first night.' Their mother was not going to give in without a fight.

'But that was only because she couldn't understand any English and she was very tired and she was very weak because in Holland they'd been half-starved in the war because the Germans took all their food and they had to eat tulip bulbs and queue up at soup kitchens and the soup was horrible with dead rats in it and cigarette-ends...'

Penny desperately wanted to go abroad more than anything else in the whole wide world. Going to visit Trudy in Holland became her dearest, her only wish. She'd even asked God in her nightly prayers to help Daddy find enough money to pay the fare on the boat. She could think of nothing else.

'We must go this year because Polly can travel for half-price,' she pointed out, frugally.

'But to impose on them so soon after the end of the war, doesn't seem quite...'

'In her letter Trudy's grown-up sister, Willy, says they don't have any rationing - or not as much as we do here where absolutely everything is still rationed. When Trudy came last year we helped her to get fat and now, if we go to Holland, we can eat as much cheese as we like and have many different sorts of milk puddings. I love milk puddings.'

'But your sister doesn't, does she?'

'Yes, I do,' said Polly because she also wanted to see Trudy again.

'We should go this year while Trudy can still remember all the English that she learned last year.'

Young children seem to be able to communicate almost by telepathy. Right from the start, the jokes and giggling between the three girls went on non-stop. Trudy had a great sense of humour and must be highly intelligent to have picked up the language so quickly. On school days, she went to classes with the other undernourished Dutch children who'd been selected to come across from Rotterdam to Tilbury to stay with families able to offer them hospitality.

Polly and Penny's home was ideal. They kept chickens and had a good vegetable garden and their mother was a good cook but those organisers of the charity must have been truly gifted salesmen. Penny could not fathom how they'd managed to persuade their mother to take in a half-starved foreigner, when she'd never met any foreigners (unless you count the

Irish or that Scottish family who lived close by.)
Polly ran away if she saw the grandfather coming
tapping along with his thick walking stick because
she couldn't understand what he said to her even
though he was talking some kind of English. - Maybe
their father had signed an agreement without asking
his wife. Penny decided her only hope of attaining
her dream was to tackle her father.

Somehow, after many days, she succeeded in
making him realise how desperately she longed to
see the world and so weeks later, there they were:
those two little schoolgirls waiting on the boat in
Rotterdam to be handed over to Willy who'd
travelled across the low, flat Netherlands to bring
them back with her to the small town not far from the
German border.


'Dear Mummy and Daddy,

Everything is marvellous and wonderful and so
interesting. The crossing was rather rough but I
wasn't seasick. Willy was waiting for us in
Rotterdam and when we got here we rushed up to
hug Trudy. She is just the same, so funny, but she's
grown a lot taller than us.

Did you know that her father was in a
concentration camp? He's very thin. His head looks
like a skull - except he has twinkly eyes just like

Trudy. He can't speak English but he made us laugh anyway.

We have a big bedroom at the front of the house. Across on the other side of the big road is a cemetery and yesterday we watched a funeral arrive, which was absolutely fantastic - very different from ones in England. There were beautiful black horses, with black plumes on their heads, pulling a black carriage with black plumes on the roof. People in black top hats and long black coats were walking in a procession. I keep hoping that another funeral will come along soon so I can improve the drawing of it I've made for you...'

The children didn't realise that they'd been given the parents' bedroom.

They loved using the washstand with the big jug of hot water. They loved absolutely everything, especially the food. Every day was a new adventure.

'... Oh no Mummy, the cemetery isn't grim at all; it's really beautiful. You can't see any of the graves from the outside. They're hidden behind weeping willows and there's a small lake with water lilies. I've done a picture for you...'

' ...Yes, I've told Polly that she must write you a letter. She says it's my fault she doesn't write. She says I've told you everything so there's no point. Yes, she's being a good girl except, the other day, she told them that they were stupid to let the Germans invade their country. I tried to explain to her that England was very lucky to have the sea as a protection. I was so embarrassed by what she'd said but Willy said I wasn't to worry.

Willy took us to a great big park or garden where there were enormous fountains shooting water high in the air and lovely flowers. You would have loved it.'

'Everyone is getting excited about Queen Wilhelmina's jubilee celebrations. All the houses have window boxes full of orange marigolds and the girls are wearing orange hair ribbons but the best thing of all - the ice cream is orange too. This is because their royal family is called the House of Orange.

Willy took us to a big church in Utrecht where we saw some ancient books chained to a lectern. They were huge manuscript bibles with most beautiful illuminations made with precious gold and blue and other colours. After the visit they bought us the orange ice creams, yum-yum!'

'Tomorrow we are allowed to go on the midnight torch procession with Trudy and her friends. We play hopscotch and ball with them in the streets behind the house. They always throw the ball to Polly, hardly ever to me. We play 'grandmother's footsteps' too.'

'The procession was fun except wax from the flaming torches dripped down onto our macs. They sang songs but of course we didn't know the words so we couldn't join in.'

'Everything is very interesting but I do feel it's not quite foreign enough. The weather and the trees are just like in England. Even this Dutch house is rather like Granny's house - sort of. I've tried to draw a picture of it because it looks just like the houses in Dutch paintings with a maid scrubbing the front step and an archway through to a small back yard where they hang up the washing.

Tomorrow we have to get up at dawn to catch a coach that is going to Amsterdam for the big celebrations. I think four coaches are going. Willy is taking us. There will be big crowds so I must keep hold of Trudy and Polly must hold Willy's hand all the time...'

'Sorry I didn't write yesterday. I was too tired because we did not get back from our big trip until nearly dawn. The coach journey was good, we could see the countryside: very green and flat with canals and the windmills turning in the wind to pump the water. We saw loads of cows. No wonder there's so much cheese and so many puddings made with milk.

I like rice pudding best. Polly is quite good at eating hers because they let her put chocolate sprinkles/gharghleslagh on it. I don't know how to spell it but I'm getting good at pronouncing the 'gh', which sounds a bit like when you're trying to cough up phlegm from the back of your throat. I try to understand their Dutch when they talk together. Sometimes I think I know what they're saying. Trudy was so clever learning English so quickly. Even if we stayed another month, I don't think I'd learn much.

Did Polly tell you about the little white dog? She loves that dog. Willy's soldier boyfriend gave it to her before he went back to Canada.

You probably want to know about the great city of Amsterdam. The best thing was the trip we took on a tourist boat through the canals at night. It was very romantic. Everything was lit up very brightly so you could see the famous houses that stand overlooking the canals. The trouble was, I kept falling asleep...

Earlier in the day we tried to get close to the royal palace to see Queen Wilhelmina and the Princesses but the crowds were so excited it was really frightening. We tried to make our way to the side of the road to escape from the crush but it took us a long time to get away. I don't like crowds.

Of course, we fell asleep on the coach coming back.

Soon we will see you again and we can tell you everything.

Thank you very much for letting us come to Holland and for paying for our fare.

Tomorrow we shall buy our presents for you.

I forgot to tell you that the presents you packed in our suitcase were greatly appreciated. Trudy loved the dress you sent which fitted her very well even though she's grown so tall. Do you remember how upset she was when someone called her dress a 'frock'? I tried to explain that it was a word some people use for children's dresses and for expensive fashionable day-dresses that aren't long evening gowns but she refused to believe me and went on crying. She felt insulted because 'frock' means something really horrible and ragged in Dutch. How tricky languages can be!

By the way, the family loved the biscuits and all the cigarettes and tobacco and the tea and sugar etc you sent - I expect Willy has written to you. She said it was a good thing that we'd had the contents of the suitcase checked and sealed by a customs officer before we left home. She might have had to pay a lot of duty on some things otherwise.

See you soon

Lots of love XXXXXXXXXXX

Penny.'

Printed in Great Britain
by Amazon